His name is
PATRICK DAWLISH

He is a very large man, six feet three inches in height, with vast shoulders that his well-cut suit cannot conceal. But for the broken nose, a legacy of an early battle in the boxing ring, he would be as handsome as he is massive.

He is always jumping in with both feet where the police fear to tread; afraid of nothing and nobody, with the possible exception of his wife Felicity. And no thief, blackmailer or murderer ever comes up against a tougher, more resourceful, deadlier enemy than

PATRICK DAWLISH.

John Creasey

as

Gordon Ashe

Death on the Move

CORGI BOOKS
A DIVISION OF TRANSWORLD PUBLISHERS

DEATH ON THE MOVE

A CORGI BOOK   552 08224 4

Originally published in Great Britain
by John Long Ltd.

PRINTING HISTORY
John Long Edition published 1945
Corgi Edition published 1969

This book is set in
Plantin 9/10 pt.

Corgi Books are published by Transworld Publishers, Ltd.,
Bashley Road, London, N.W.10

Made and printed in Great Britain by
Richard Clay (The Chaucer Press), Ltd., Bungay, Suffolk

A MAN NAMED DAWLISH

In 1939 John Creasey lived in a village called 'Ashe' in Hampshire. There he created Patrick Dawlish and his pseudonym of Gordon Ashe. Dawlish was shown as a huge man with a group of hearty hard-hitting friends, based on the 'Bulldog Drummond' tradition. He was drawn by chance into a vicious series of crime, and decided to solve it himself. This brought him into conflict with the law, represented by (then) Chief Inspector William Trivett. Trivett had much more sympathy than most policemen would have had with this tremendous personality whose 'hunches' were really a logical development of ideas, linked together with bewildering speed.

Soon, the war brought a new challenge. Patrick Dawlish became a powerful and far-famed figure in MI5—Britain's Intelligence Corps. He dropped into occupied Europe countless times—organising resistance, sabotage, against the hated Nazis. And, spiriting prisoner after prisoner across the English Channel he became renowned as a modern Scarlet Pimpernel. During these dangerous, desperate war-time days, he met and married Felicity; and Trivett (now Superintendent) was able to help him officially in many of his exploits.

The end of the war sent Dawlish into enforced retirement, with his beloved Felicity. He tried to settle down to the peaceful life of the English countryside, rearing pigs and fowls and growing apples. He no longer went looking for trouble, but trouble sought him out. He became a kind of unpaid private eye—and often found himself in conflict with the police; and Trivett! Felicity had little patience with his anti-crime activities but eventually, like Trivett, she came to the conclusion that this was the life he both loved and needed. He hated crime and instinctively wanted to help anyone in danger or in trouble.

Then out of the blue he was invited to become a Deputy Assistant Commissioner for Crime at Scotland Yard, his special task to fight any crime which crossed national and conventional borders. He was Britain's delegate to a world Police Convention which was in constant session—and soon the world came to know these fierce, dauntless, dedicated fighters against crime as *The Crime Haters*.

Soon, too, Dawlish became the dominant figure in the organisation, with Felicity's full understanding and support. While Trivett, although in a different branch of the C.I.D., grew used to the strange irony that his old friend-cum-adversary was now his chief!

CHAPTER ONE

THE REPUTATION OF MAJOR DAWLISH

'YOU see that large man in uniform, sitting by the window,' said the fluffy-haired woman who was having tea with a youthful lieutenant at Penrod's. 'No, not *that* one, you ass, the fair-haired man!'

The lieutenant shifted his glance a little resentfully.

'He's Patrick Dawlish—and absolutely marvellous!'

The fluffy-haired woman uttered the name in a hushed tone, but the 'marvellous' had attracted attention. Major Patrick Dawlish became aware of the gaze from a dozen pairs of eyes.

'If it weren't for that broken nose,' the fluffy-haired one went on dreamily, 'he'd be *divine*! I expect he's waiting for a friend who hasn't turned up yet.' She looked as if she would like to go and comfort him, but he turned his gaze towards her and it was so blank that she went on hurriedly: 'It isn't only his looks, Willy. He's so famous! Even before the war he was always *doing* something, and his name has been in the papers a great deal since then. I remember, it was about six months ago, when there was that mysterious business in Devon or Dorset or somewhere down in the West country. Some Nazis had landed in England, or something or other, and he——'

She went on and on, her voice low-pitched but penetrating. Dawlish, now smoking his third cigarette since four o'clock, the time when Felicity, his wife, should have been there to meet him, was aware of the covert glances and had some idea of what the fluffy-haired woman was saying.

Fame, Dawlish was apt to say, had been thrust upon him, and he found it a poor substitute for greatness. He had a mild sense of grievance; what he had considered to be one or two innocent adventures before the war had brought him into contact with the police and crime. He had a curious ability to get to the heart of whatever attracted his attention, and to ignore inessentials. After two such adventures he had decided on a quiet life, only to be drawn into greater activity—twice at the instigation of the police themselves. When the war had come he had imagined that the days of public attention were past and that his only action would be abroad. Instead he had been drawn into operations at home. Becoming one of the leading lights in a small branch of Secret Intelligence.

In fact, wherever there was trouble there was Dawlish. At one time he had looked upon these incidents in an amused manner, but they no longer amused him.

He was more aggrieved because his reputation had undoubtedly been responsible for his being stationed in England when he had longed to be sent abroad.

That afternoon, however, nothing worried him but the fact that Felicity was late. She so rarely was.

At twenty minutes to five, the waitress approached him.

'Would you like your tea now, sir?'

'I'll wait another ten minutes,' smiled Dawlish.

The lieutenant and the fluffy-haired woman were getting up to go. Their departure coincided with the flurried entrance of a girl in A.T.S. uniform.

The lieutenant turned to watch her as she floundered towards Major Dawlish, heedless of his companion's tug on his arm.

'Willy!'

'Sorry,' he apologised quickly.

'What has come over you?' she demanded.

'Now listen——' he began, but stopped abruptly and looked at a man who was standing near the kerb. There was nothing remarkable about the fellow, except that he was breathing heavily and his lank hair was ruffled; like the A.T.S. girl, he had been hurrying.

'Willy, *what*——'

'Darling, I may have to dash off and leave you,' said 'Willy' in an undertone. 'Don't look round, there's a pet.' There was a light note in his voice, but beneath it a certain jubilance. 'I fancy that something odd is going on,' he added. 'You'll help enormously if you'll nip over to that tobacconist and buy some cigarettes.'

Surprised and startled, she complied while Willy gave all his attention to the man standing on the kerb. The fellow was glancing along the road, the hands lighting a cigarette, visibly shaking. 'Willy' stepped into a nearby porch and watched him.

A car drew up alongside, and the man's face cleared. When

8

the occupant of the car opened the window, he jerked his thumb over his shoulder.

As the window was closed a rather high-pitched voice drifted through it.

'Well, it can't be helped. Don't lose him.'

It was the voice of a fat man, and the impression was heightened by a glimpse of humped shoulders and a double chin.

As the car moved off, Dawlish came out of the restaurant, the A.T.S. girl by his side. They passed the young lieutenant. Unnoticed, the man on the kerb began to follow them.

Willy moved swiftly along to the tobacconist and gripped the fluffy-haired woman's arm.

'Sorry, pet, but I can't come back now. Meet me at Pam's for a cocktail and I'll tell you all about it then.' He hesitated, and then hissed into her startled ear: 'It's to do with Dawlish.'

He strode after the agitated man, who himself was following Dawlish and the A.T.S. girl.

It looked as if Dawlish was going to walk down to the towing-path and along the river bank, when suddenly he took his companion's elbow and hurried across the road. It happened so swiftly that the lank-haired man was completely taken aback. There was traffic coming in each direction; for Dawlish had chosen a moment when he and his companion could get across but could not be followed.

By the time his two followers had reached the opposite pavement, Dawlish had disappeared. There were several turnings he could have taken and a dozen shops into which he could have gone.

The lank-haired man gave up at last, and began to walk away.

'Willy' decided to follow him.

Both boarded a bus and alighted at the top of Putney Hill. One discreetly behind the other, they walked across the edge of Wimbledon Common, towards the grounds of a block of flats. The lank-haired man walked round to the back entrance and disappeared, while 'Willy', not certain what to do, hesitated and then decided to wait. By the time he had noted that the flats were named 'Hillcrest' and that the plaques outside said: 'Numbers 1–41', a car drew up and he caught another glimpse of the man with the double chin.

He did not see the owner of the chins glance round and peer

9

at him through the rear-window. Thinking himself unobserved, he sauntered across the road towards the common and took up a position by a clump of bushes from which he could see the front entrance to the flats. By now the fat man had entered the building.

'I wonder if I'm being a fool?' mused 'Willy'. He lit a cigarette and prepared to wait.

If he had moved to the right or to the left, he would have been saved, but he stood still. The bullet which came from the window of the fat man's flat caught him in the forehead, and he died instantaneously. He fell forward, and had been lying still for several minutes before a child running after a ball suddenly turned and fled, screaming:

'Mummy—*Mummy!*'

CHAPTER TWO

FELICITY'S BRIGHT IDEA

WHEN Dawlish said that fame had been thrust upon him, implying that the police were solely responsible, he overlooked a characteristic trait which had intrigued certain officers at Scotland Yard from the moment they had first met the large, impassive-looking man with the blue eyes and indolent manner. That characteristic trait was his ability to see past inessentials.

That afternoon was a case in point.

The plump A.T.S. girl had told him, in a whisper, that Captain Dawlish (she meant Felicity) had sent her to ask him to go with her. Immediately they had reached the street he had seen the lank-haired man, and quickly realised what the fellow was doing. He had also noticed the youthful lieutenant.

Once safe from pursuit, he had looked down on the A.T.S. girl with a smile. 'I'm sorry about the rush,' he said, 'but I wanted to make sure that no one followed us. Now, what is it all about?'

'I don't really know, sir,' said the girl. 'Only that Captain Dawlish told me where you were and asked me to fetch you as quickly as I could. I'm Sergeant Winneger, sir.'

'We'll soon find out more about it,' Dawlish assured her.

For Felicity to be late and then to send an urgent message had been quite enough to make him act first and ask questions afterwards; but he wished he could have followed the lank-haired man. That was his only regret as he approached the camp, a small one on the outskirts of Kingston.

The main entrance was guarded, but Sergeant Winneger led him straight past it, along a narrow road. There was open ground on one side and a fringe of trees in the distance; strong barbed-wire entanglements protected the side abutting on the camp. A series of low buildings and huts were all that could be seen above the hedge on which the barbed-wire was fixed.

'It's not far along here,' said Sergeant Winneger, as they approached a corner.

Turning it, they came upon a little crowd of uniformed people, an ambulance and a small private car.

Almost at once Dawlish saw his wife.

She was talking to a hard-faced Colonel.

On the ground was the body of a girl which two men were about to lift on to a stretcher. Only the head and shoulders of the girl were visible, for she was covered in blankets, but it was possible to see that she was in uniform. Felicity, now finished with her C.O., turned to Dawlish, her grey-green eyes sombre.

'What's the trouble?' he asked gently.

'I think she'll die,' said Felicity, 'so you can call it murder.' She sounded a little distraught. 'Let's get away. If there had been anything for you to see near the spot it would be trampled on by now.' She led the way further along the narrow road. Soon, they were out of earshot of the crowd. Only the sound of the ambulance engine came to them.

Felicity gripped Dawlish's arm tightly. She had been with him through too many fierce adventures to be so affected by murder. Presumably, therefore, there was something else on her mind. Dawlish did not ask questions. In her own good time, she would tell him.

The lane led to a stretch of common-land with trees and bushes on either side. Near one of them Felicity stopped abruptly and flashed an unexpected smile.

'I *must* tidy up!' she said.

'Undoubtedly,' said Dawlish, gravely.

He held her small mirror in position while she ran her comb

through her hair, and put her forage cap on again at the correct angle. He was still in love with her, and knew that he always would be.

'Better?'

'Much!' he kissed her forehead. 'You don't happen to know of a handy place where we can get some tea, do you?'

'Poor sweet!' said Felicity, 'I'd forgotten you missed lunch. I think there is a cottage along here where they used to do teas.' She lengthened her stride. 'Pat, it's the second murder near the camp.'

'Yes, I remembered that,' said Dawlish.

'Two months ago,' went on Felicity, rapidly, 'and it looked like—I mean, everyone thought that it was one of the sordid affairs which *do* happen from time to time. It was late at night, after a dance, and the girl who was murdered had drunk too much. So had the man they arrested, I think. He wasn't caught for three weeks, and I don't know where he is now.'

'At Brixton,' said Dawlish.

She glanced up at him sharply.

'Have you followed the case?'

'Only because it happened near you,' said Dawlish. 'I haven't evolved any elaborate ideas about . . .'

'Well, there was one rather queer thing about it,' went on Felicity, 'the murdered girl had a fresh tattoo mark on her right shoulder, near the neck——'

'A tiny five-point star with a circle in the middle,' said Dawlish, promptly.

'You haven't forgotten much,' commented Felicity. 'No one could explain it, and it didn't seem particularly important. The only other thing was that the man they arrested said that he quarrelled with her and left her near the copse. It seemed, at the time, a pretty weak story.'

'The police certainly thought so,' agreed Dawlish.

'I did, too,' Felicity admitted, 'but now—Pat, this girl has the same tattoo mark.'

'Wasn't she fully dressed?' asked Dawlish sharply.

'Oh, yes, but I was in the wash-room with her two days ago and noticed the mark then. Another strange thing is that she and the other girl were good friends. Looking back, Pat, I know that I was a fool to accept the surface explanation so readily. For she wasn't a girl to get drunk. She was steady and am-

12

bitious like Mary Hill.'

'This one is Mary Hill?'

'Yes. Neither of them were heavy drinkers, and I was surprised when I heard that she had been drunk that night. I thought the man who killed her first plied her with drinks and made her lose her head, but now——'

'The fellow's only accused of killing her, so far,' protested Dawlish. 'I think I read somewhere that the trial's coming off next week.'

'Oh, well, perhaps I'm making a fuss about nothing,' said Felicity, 'but I did see a rather furtive-looking fellow hanging round the scene of the crime. I rather hoped that you would be here before he went away.'

'Did he have dark, lank hair and a hang-dog look about him?' inquired Dawlish airily.

'He most certainly *did*!'

'Then he followed your Sergeant Winneger, and then tried to follow me. Did he overhear my name?'

'Almost sure to have done,' said Felicity. 'I called out instructions—to go to Penrod's and fetch Major Dawlish—fairly loudly.'

'Now why on earth should he chase after your girl because she was going for me?' asked Dawlish. They walked on in silence until they came to the cottage with a weather-beaten sign reading: *Teas*. Gloomily eating and drinking the stale sandwiches and stewed tea served to them, they were glad to leave the musty parlour and get back to the fresh air again.

Felicity had forty-eight hours leave and Dawlish was off duty until the following evening, so they decided to catch the seven o'clock train to Waterloo. The clock struck a quarter to eight as they reached their small furnished flat in Brook Street.

'What would you like to do now?' asked Felicity.

'I don't know,' admitted Dawlish, restlessly: 'I do know that the murder—or attempted murder, she isn't dead yet—of Mary Hill has rather damped our spirits. Too bad on a forty-eight! Would you care to go out and drown your sorrows somewhere?'

Felicity shook her head. 'Do you know, I think I'll put a call through to the camp and see how she is.'

The connection took some little time, then Dawlish heard her ask the question uppermost on her mind, and knew from her expression that the answer was distressing.

He was aware of a curious blanket of depression.

He had never met Mary Hill, so it was not the fact that the girl had died that worried him. The incident of the dark-haired man was puzzling, but nothing more. As it was, he found himself thinking of the soldier who was under arrest on the charge of the murder of the first girl. He could not recall the man's name, although he remembered the circumstances clearly.

'The truth is,' said Dawlish abruptly, 'that I ought to have a word with Bill.'

'If you do get in touch with Scotland Yard, you might be drawn into some pretty devilish goings on,' said Felicity. 'Do you want to be?'

'Not much,' said Dawlish, 'but even so, I think I'll see if Bill's at the Yard.'

Superintendent William Trivett, a friend of many years, was not at Scotland Yard, and nor was he at his home. His wife answered Dawlish from the Chelsea house, saying that he had telephoned from Kingston to say that he would not be home until late. Dawlish thanked her, and rang off. He looked significantly at Felicity.

'Bill's already at Kingston.'

A ring at the front doorbell interrupted his words.

'I'll go,' said Felicity. Dawlish stood smoking by the window, still conscious of the depressing effect of what had happened. Then he heard a feminine voice which he recognised immediately. He was staring towards the door when Felicity admitted the fluffy-haired woman of the tea-shop. She looked agitated, and she had not changed from her suit of bright green linen.

'Do forgive this intrusion, Major Dawlish,' she said. 'You may possibly recall having seen me at Penrod's this afternoon.'

'I do, very well,' said Dawlish, wondering what on earth had prompted her visit. She was pretty, but not startlingly so. Dawlish put her down as thirty-five, and thought that he might be four or five years on the generous side at that. 'It's such a *curious* business. Willy—Lieutenant Carr, who was with me this afternoon . . .'

She talked at some length, eagerly.

She said she had come to Dawlish because 'Willy' had not met her at Pam's, a West End club, as arranged. His last words had been that he had gone off on his own because of something to do with Dawlish. She remembered that she had told Carr

14

something of what she knew of Dawlish's reputation. *Did* Major Dawlish happen to know where he was?

The telephone's sharp ring interrupted Dawlish's assurance that he had never heard of Carr.

Felicity answered it. A rather prim voice inquired if Mrs. Desmond were there. The fluffy-haired woman looked up at once.

'That will be Agnes!' she exclaimed, 'my maid—I told her where I was coming, and to call me if Lieutenant Carr telephoned for me. Oh, what a relief! Yes, Agnes . . .'

There was a long pause.

Dawlish and Felicity saw her face drain of its colour as she replaced the receiver. Willy, she said in a low, vibrant voice, had been murdered; a friend had just telephoned the news to her maid.

As she dropped into a chair, the front doorbell rang again.

CHAPTER THREE

SUPERINTENDENT TRIVETT

This time Dawlish opened the door.

He was not really surprised to see Superintendent Trivett standing there.

'Hallo, Pat—I hoped you'd be in.'

'I hoped you would telephone,' said Dawlish, drawing him into the hall. 'Don't give your name, or rather, your rank. I've someone here with a curious story. On second thoughts,' he added, 'we'd better have a word or two on our own.'

He led the way into the bedroom, closed the door and sat on the edge of the bed as Trivett took the only easy-chair. 'Do you know anything about a man named Carr—Lieutenant Carr?'

Trivett said: 'A Lieutenant Carr was killed on Wimbledon Common this afternoon.'

'Is that all you know about him?'

'Yes, except that he was in the Tank Corps,' said Trivett. He looked at Dawlish curiously. 'I came to have a word with you about a different business, the murder of an A.T.S. girl at

Kingston. Are these two things connected?'

'In some strange way, I think they are,' said Dawlish. 'What made you come?'

'The C.O. said that you'd been on the spot,' said Trivett, 'and I wondered why.'

Clearly, and to the point, Dawlish proceeded to tell him.

Trivett listened with marked attention. 'Well, what do you make of it?'

Dawlish said: 'It looks as if Carr put two and two together, and because Mrs. Desmond had aroused his curiosity about me, he plunged off in the wake of the lank-haired man. I saw him haring along.'

Trivett looked thoughtful.

'Would Carr have jumped to it as quickly as that?'

'I think he did,' said Dawlish. 'He told his companion that he was doing something connected with me, and as I'd never heard of him, it must have been on the spur of the moment.' When Trivett continued to look doubtful, Dawlish added: 'It's possible that Carr had some prior knowledge—is that what's on your mind?'

'Yes. It's hardly likely that he was murdered because he followed the dark-haired man, is it?'

'No,' said Dawlish, 'but it's possible that he was murdered because he found where the dark-haired merchant went.' He rubbed the bridge of his broken nose. 'I think you'd better cut out any idea that Carr was associated with this business in any way except a casual one. The likeliest theory is that he followed the dark-haired man to Wimbledon Common, and saw where he went.'

'Would anyone commit murder for such a motive?'

Dawlish shrugged. 'I think someone did, but you needn't take it for granted. You'll check on Carr's recent movements, of course, and you may as well check on Mrs. Desmond's. Felicity thought that the dark-haired merchant looked up to no good, and she isn't a bad judge. He was near the scene of the murder and he looked agitated when I saw him. That seems to tie up. The murdered girl had the tattoo mark—you've heard about it before, I suppose?'

'Yes, she's the second girl with a similar mark to be murdered near that camp. They were both in the Stores Depot. That's why Felicity sent for you, isn't it?' Dawlish nodded, and Trivett went on: 'Seriously, Pat, do you know anything else?'

'Absolutely nothing,' said Dawlish.

'You haven't been following up the first murder?'

'I know most of what there is to know about it,' Dawlish said, 'but only because I was curious.' He grinned. 'What about the man you've charged with the first murder? Is the case a strong one?'

'Circumstantially it can't be broken,' admitted Trivett, 'but usually there's a background to support the case. In this one, there isn't. Penrose appears to be a decent enough fellow, neither a heavy drinker nor a womaniser. He's admitted that he did quarrel with the girl a short while before she was murdered, and even admits that she slapped his face. His cap fell off, and he was in such a rage, he says, that he didn't trouble to pick it up. It was found near the body, and was the first thing which put us on to him. His employers believe in him and are paying for his defence. To tell you the truth, I haven't been too happy about the case. After this later development I hope to persuade the others to hold it up for a bit.'

By 'the others', Dawlish knew, he meant his seniors at the Yard. Dawlish also knew that it would not be easy.

'When is Penrose down for trial?' he asked.

'Next week.'

'Why not let it go through?' asked Dawlish, thoughtfully. 'If you get it postponed you'll tell whoever did the murder that there's some doubt, and might put him on his guard.' He smiled faintly. 'Doesn't that appeal to you?'

'I don't like to think of any innocent man standing trial for murder,' said Trivett.

'One man's torment might save several lives,' answered Dawlish soberly. 'Let's face it, Bill. There have been two murders, and the tattoo mark suggests that they're connected, apart from the fact that members of the personnel at the same camp were the victims. Even without the tattoo mark on Mary Hill's shoulder, the dark-haired customer and the murder of Carr would make it unusual. How was Carr killed?'

'He was shot through the head, probably from some distance away.'

'Well, there's your justification,' said Dawlish. 'Cold-blooded murder of a man who stumbled across some information and the equally cold-blooded murder of two A.T.S. girls. It's quite a business. Go ahead with Penrose's trial,' he added, and grinned. 'If I were you, I would have a word with the Press, too, and ask them to give it plenty of publicity, on the lines of: "The Safety of Our Service Girls Must Be Ensured." Focus attention on the trial of Penrose, connect it with the murder of Mary Hill, but only as another Awful Example.' Although he continued to smile and his words were ironic, they had an undercurrent of seriousness. 'You could even get the Press to elaborate it, and put out one or two statements about a hunt for a soldier seen near the camp this afternoon. Or is that asking too much of an honest policeman?'

'There are times when you horrify me,' Trivett said. 'I'll think about it, Pat. Meanwhile, what are you going to do?'

'I don't know,' said Dawlish. 'A polite word to my C.O. would probably get me a week or ten days leave.'

'In other words, you want to come in?'

'I do, rather,' admitted Dawlish. 'They were two nice girls, according to Felicity, and apart from that there are intriguing points, aren't there? But if I do get leave, William, I don't want to be tied down by regulations. If I'm to do any good, I need to be a free agent.'

'I'll see what I can do,' Trivett promised. 'Meanwhile, what about Mrs. Desmond?'

'Must you see her now?'

'I needn't.'

'Visit her when she gets home, and don't let on that there's any connection between you and me,' suggested Dawlish. 'Meanwhile give me a ring, as soon as you can, about my leave, will you?'

Trivett nodded agreement. He was a little uneasy and Dawlish was aware of it. Aware, too, that Archibald Morely the Assistant Commissioner's approval must be sought, as also that of his own C.O. It should not be too difficult, decided Dawlish, as he went in to see Mrs. Desmond.

She was composed enough, though it was obvious that she had not fully recovered from the shock. She was sipping a cup of tea, and Felicity was having one with her. Dawlish sauntered across the room and leaned against the window.

'I still *can't* believe it,' said Mrs. Desmond.

'It's always difficult to believe in sudden death,' said Dawlish, 'but refusing to do so won't help us, I'm afraid.' His manner softened the harshness of the words. 'Did you notice anything at or near Penrod's which might explain why he hurried after me, Mrs. Desmond?'

'No, *nothing*, nothing at all!'

She reiterated that at some length, but in the course of half an hour, several things emerged. The fact that the dark-haired man had intrigued Carr was one, and another was the mention of a motor-car which had pulled up. He heard, also, of the fat man who had been in the back of the car; when pressed, Mrs. Desmond *thought* that the car had been a taxi or a hackney-carriage; vaguely, she remembered the hackney-carriage plate at the back of the car.

When she left, Dawlish telephoned Scotland Yard. Trivett was not in his office, and Dawlish left a message about the fat man and the hackney-carriage. It was getting dark by then, and Dawlish declared that nothing more could be done that night. 'Let's go to the club, shall we?'

'You mean, let's give you a chance for a get-together with Ted or Tim, don't you?' said Felicity dryly.

They reached the Clayton Club a little after nine o'clock. Although it was not a Service Club it was popular with Service men. At that time, a large number of officers and men were in London, at a loose end, and Dawlish knew that two of his close friends, Timothy Jeremy and Edward Beresford, were likely to be there. He had not been in the club for more than five minutes before he saw the large and ungainly bulk of Beresford in one armchair, and the thin, almost gaunt face of Jeremy in another.

They drew up chairs and talked happily of this and that, until Dawlish hinted that he had something of importance to say; thereafter, they listened with keen attention. Their interest quickened when Dawlish took an envelope from his pocket and sketched a five-point star with a circle inside it.

CHAPTER FOUR

PERMISSION TO ACT

WHILE Dawlish and his friends were talking in the Clayton
Club, Trivett and the Assistant Commissioner were talking in
the latter's room at Scotland Yard. Morely had put in an
appearance after being advised of the two murders, which at
first sight appeared to be unconnected. When he heard what
Dawlish had said, he eyed Trivett ruefully.

'So Dawlish is at it again.'

'He assured me that he knew nothing more than he's told me,'
Trivett told his chief, 'and I'm inclined to believe him. Actually
I don't think it matters much whether he knows anything more
or not, sir. Do you?'

'You're probably right,' conceded Morely. 'You want him in,
do you?'

'Yes,' said Trivett.

'Because he might know something, or——' Morely paused.

'Because he's a comfortable man to have with us,' said
Trivett, frankly. 'If he's right and this is a big business, we won't
be sorry to have him.'

'He has been known to be wrong,' said Morely dryly.

'He's been right far more often,' insisted Trivett doggedly.
'Will you have a word with the Intelligence Department, sir?'

It was remarkable that Trivett felt so certain, and even more
remarkable that Morely raised no objections. He immediately
dialled the number of Colonel Whitehead, Dawlish's C.O. A
brief conversation ensued, followed by a chuckle.

'Let's say he's been working pretty hard for the past few
weeks. If you can use him, go ahead.'

'Will you tell him that he's got leave?'

'Certainly,' said Whitehead, 'and I also warn you here and
now that the chances of you getting Beresford and Jeremy as
well are heavily in your favour. Or does the thought of the trio
frighten you?'

'We'll bear up,' said Morely.

Later that night the necessary chits were sent by messenger to
the three men. That, Dawlish said, really started the affair of
the curious tattoo mark.

Her friends believed that Laura Desmond was both shocked and acutely disappointed by the murder of Willy Carr. She had the reputation of getting everything she wanted, and few doubted that she had counted on Willy as her second husband.

Trivett was prepared to find her nervous and on edge. Nevertheless, he judged her to be more intelligent than her reputation suggested, and detailed a Sergeant Munk to watch her Mayfair flat.

As he gave instructions, Trivett wondered why Dawlish had suggested so casually that he should keep an eye on Mrs. Desmond.

'What I want to know,' said Munk, who treated his senior with conventional respect when others were present, but was fractious when they were alone, 'is what happens if Dawlish or any of his big hams come along?'

'Don't interfere unless you have to,' said Trivett.

'So that's it,' grumbled Munk. 'You're just letting him have his own way again, as usual. One of these days you'll be sorry.' He sniffed.

He sniffed again as he watched his Chief disappearing into the gloom of Bethel Street. There was no moon, but the stars were out and it was possible to see across the road. As soon as Trivett was out of sight, Munk's features relaxed. He grinned as he selected the site of bombed premises for watching Mrs. Desmond's flat. He had, in fact, a great affection and admiration for Dawlish, although only once in the six years of their assocation had he even remotely admitted it.

The time was a little after ten-thirty.

A man walked leisurely along Bethel Street, which was short and narrow, with only a dozen houses which remained inhabitable. Munk watched him, and smiled faintly. The newcomer disappeared, but soon walked back again. Munk's grin widened, for he had recognised Ted Beresford.

'They're smart,' thought Munk, 'no doubt about that, they're smart! He's seen me.'

Ted Beresford, in fact, suspected that there was a man standing in the shadows. He chose that spot to light a cigarette, and by the flare of the match he saw Munk, but did not recognise him. He sauntered further along the street and stood in the porchway of a house, wondering whether Trivett had a man watching Mrs. Desmond, or whether a third party was

21

interested in her.

Just after eleven o'clock a taxi drew up near Mrs. Desmond's flat. A figure alighted.

Munk, who possessed an almost photographic memory and was used to working after dark, managed to see the number in the red glow of the rear lamp. The taxi moved off, and the newcomer slipped into the house where Laura Desmond lived. Munk did not move. Beresford went quickly towards the flats, but instead of going in, as Munk expected, turned and made a bee-line for the sergeant. Before Munk could do anything, Beresford shone a torch into his startled eyes.

' 'Ere——' began Munk.

'What ho!' said Beresford, keeping his voice low. 'So it's you, is it! I'll toss you who goes up.'

'Up where?' growled Munk, who did not like being taken at a disadvantage.

'Be reasonable,' begged Beresford. 'We can't both go to see what Laura's doing, now can we? All right, if you're nervous, I'll go.' He turned and retraced his steps, and Munk glared at him, breathing: *'Nervous! Me!'*

Beresford slipped into the house and up the carpeted stairs.

He already knew that Laura Desmond's flat was number 5, and when he reached the door he saw a light beneath it and heard her voice. Beresford glanced over his shoulder, feeling fairly sure that Munk would be tactful enough not to come upon him unawares. He took a pen-knife from his pocket and in a few minutes he had picked the lock.

Beresford closed the door softly and approached the only room where a light was now shining.

He could distinguish Laura Desmond's words.

'No,' she was saying, 'I've never heard the name. And I shall telephone for the police if you don't go!'

'What a brave little woman you are,' sneered a man's voice. 'But I want the truth, and I intend to have it. You were seen going into his flat.'

'I——' began Laura, 'I——'

Beresford stood just outside the door, visualising the scene. The woman was being asked whether she knew Dawlish.

'Now, the truth!' The man's voice was threatening, although it was pitched on a low key. 'What did you tell Dawlish? Come on, answer me!'

22

'I——' she began again, and broke off.

Beresford heard the sound of a sharp slap.

He opened the door an inch, but could not see into the room.

Suddenly, Laura Desmond broke down and began to talk; her story was the same as the one Dawlish had already reported. There was a frightened note in her voice which rose to a gasp of hysteria.

'That—that's all,' she cried, 'I can't tell you any more, I've told you everything.'

'I wonder if you have,' said the man.

'I tell you——'

Laura Desmond's voice stopped, and she caught her breath. Beresford, judging the moment ripe, pushed the door open and stepped through, but neither of the others saw him. The man's back was towards him, and he could just see Laura Desmond's face and her eyes, distended with a fear so acute that Beresford stopped momentarily. Then he took another step forward and saw the automatic in the man's hand.

'Good evening,' he said.

The man with the gun spun round, and at that moment Beresford struck him. He reeled back, but kept his hold on the gun. Beresford stretched out a long arm, caught his wrist and twisted it. Both the gun and the man fell to the floor.

Laura Desmond staggered to a chair and dropped into it.

Beresford picked up the gun and, holding it gingerly by the muzzle, glanced at the man and then the woman. He stepped to the telephone and dialled Dawlish's number, noting as he did so that the dazed look on the fallen man's face had been replaced by one more calculating. Beresford put the automatic, a small one with a mother-of-pearl handle, on to the table next to the telephone and took out a much more powerful-looking gun. With that he covered the man on the floor.

'Dawlish speaking,' said Dawlish, into his ear.

'Pat, we've made a strike,' drawled Beresford. 'Can you come over at once? ... Yes, her flat ... By the way, Munk's outside ... Good!'

The man was now struggling up, and seemed prepared to bolt for the door.

Beresford shook his head; he was a plain man, and some people called him ugly. Others said that his features were

23

redeemed by his smile; but he was not smiling now.

'No go,' he said, 'we have things to say. What's your name?'

'Who—who are you?' demanded the other, taking a deep breath.

'I'm asking the questions,' said Beresford, 'and I want answers. What's your name?'

It was Laura Desmond who answered, surprising him enough to make him glance at her, which was a foolish thing to do.

'He said his name was Smith,' she said.

'Smith, eh?' said Beresford.

He broke off, for 'Smith' made a dive for the door. He was half-way there when Beresford stuck out a leg and tripped him up. The man who called himself Smith did not try to get up again, but Beresford was taking no more chances.

'Take his wallet out of his pocket, will you?' he said pleasantly to Laura.

'His—his *wallet*!'

'Temporarily, of course. I'll give it back to him.'

Seeing the cruel marks on her face and throat, Beresford watched with sympathy her frightened approach, and the terrified hand stretched gingerly towards the man's coat. Either Smith had hurt himself in his fall or he was foxing; he made no move as Mrs. Desmond removed the wallet, then backed hastily away.

'You know, you're good at this,' said Beresford with a congratulatory note in his voice, 'our Mr. Smith hardly knew that it happened.'

Laura moved purposefully towards a cabinet and took out a whisky decanter and two glasses.

'Not for me, thanks,' said Beresford hastily, 'I'm on duty. Don't take too much yourself, either,' he added severely. 'Look here, let me pour you out a drink!'

Laura accepted the weak whisky-and-soda which Beresford poured out for her, and drank it meekly. There followed a brief period of inaction, but before long, footsteps sounded on the stairs.

'That will be Dawlish,' said Beresford, after a moment's intense listening. 'You can let him in.'

She opened the door and Dawlish strode forward, conscious that in his pocket reposed the chit from his C.O. authorising him to consider himself on leave, as from nine o'clock that evening. That may have accounted for the satisfied smile on his face as he beamed at Mrs. Desmond and then at the man who was on the floor.

'Hallo,' he said, 'what's the matter? Hurt yourself?'

'Dawlish,' began the man, and then stopped.

'Yes,' said Dawlish, encouragingly.

'You——' began the man on the floor, and stopped again.

'He must be shy,' said Dawlish. 'What happened?'

'He came, he threatened, he asked all about you, and was about to use that little toy on the table,' said Beresford. 'I had to dot him one.'

Dawlish picked up the wallet. 'His?'

'Yes. I haven't looked inside.'

'Praiseworthy restraint,' said Dawlish. He opened the wallet. Two letters, several visiting cards, about twenty pounds in one-pound notes, a book of stamps, a registration card, a driving licence and a personal points sheet, followed each other in neat array on to the table. Both letters were addressed to *Bertram Smythe, 44 Hillcrest Court, Putney,* the name and address on the registration card. Dawlish did not even bat an eyelash.

He looked into every compartment of the wallet and found them empty. As he did so, he glanced at Bertram Smythe, and he saw from the man's tension that he was still afraid that the wallet might yield some secret of importance. Dawlish pulled out the lining of two of the compartments. The lining on one of the compartments was fitted with a small zip fastener. He opened it, then shook the wallet again. Three cards, the size and shape of visiting cards, fell to the table. Dawlish glanced at Smythe and saw the man's pallor. Then he picked up a card which was blank on one side, turned it over and saw only one thing. There was no name or address, but in the top left-hand corner was a small five-point star, with a tiny circle in the middle.

25

CHAPTER FIVE

THE OBSTINACY OF MR. SMYTHE

'CURIOUS things,' said Dawlish, inspecting the cards as if he had never seen anything like them. He nodded to Beresford, who lugged the man to his feet and pushed him into an easy-chair. All this Laura Desmond watched with rounded eyes. The astonishing nonchalance of the two large men appeared to have given her confidence.

Smythe's breath came out as if from a punctured tyre as he dropped into the chair.

'Why were you worried about them?' Dawlish said abruptly.

Smythe did not speak.

Dawlish loomed over him, frowning. Smythe stared up at the two massive men, and set his lips.

Beresford said in a conversational way; 'He nearly strangled Mrs. Desmond.'

'*We* don't want to strangle *him*—unless we have to,' Dawlish said regretfully. 'What do these cards mean, Smythe?'

'I won't tell you,' said Smythe hoarsely, 'and you can't make me.'

'Brave words, but foolish,' said Dawlish.

Methodically, he went through a string of questions, but Smythe remained mute. At last, Dawlish gave up and turned to Beresford.

'We can't work on him here, he'll have to wait.' He went to the telephone and dialled Whitehall 1212, asking for Trivett, who was not in. He dialled Trivett's home number and the Superintendent answered at once.

'Not in bed yet?' asked Dawlish. 'Good. I've a job for you. Carr—you remember Carr?'

'Go on,' snapped Trivett.

'He was probably shot from the window of 44 Hillcrest Court, Putney Hill,' said Dawlish. He did not appear to be looking at Smythe, but actually he could see him out of the corner of his eye. 'If you get there quickly you'll probably pick up the fat man, and that would be useful.'

Smythe started.

'Are you sure?' demanded Trivett.

'As near as makes no difference,' Dawlish assured him. 'By the way, a man named Bertram Smythe, who lives at the flat or has an address there, looked in to see Mrs. Desmond tonight. He got away by the back door.'

Trivett did not seem unduly cast down by this news; probably, thought Dawlish, he knew well enough that Smythe had not got away, and that Dawlish was simply observing the rules. He rang off, glancing obliquely at Mrs. Desmond.

'But he's still here!' Laura Desmond cried in astonishment.

'Dear me, how forgetful of me. So he is. Well, we certainly can't hand him over to the police now! So that gives us a free hand with which to make him talk.'

Smythe was beginning to sweat, his hands moving unsteadily in a war of nerves, Dawlish was an artist, and he did not think it would be very long before Smythe broke. The longer he was left alone, and the more veiled the threats, the quicker the results were likely to be. Dawlish lit a cigarette, and glanced again at the contents of the wallet. When he took out the letters, Smythe did nothing to suggest that he minded Dawlish reading them. One was from a woman who addressed him in affectionate terms. It was dated a few days before, but there was no address. The second letter was typewritten on the stationery of an obscure firm of biscuit manufacturers; it confirmed an appointment with Smythe for later in the week.

Dawlish put the letters down, and turned to Laura Desmond.

'You won't feel too happy on your own here, tonight,' he said, 'perhaps you'd like to go to my flat and keep my wife company?' He was dialling as he spoke, and Felicity answered. 'Hallo, my sweet! I'd like Tim to come over to bring Laura Desmond to the flat. Is that OK? Look after her, won't you?'

He listened with a broad smile for a moment or two, and then replaced the receiver.

Dawlish put out a hand and picked up the small automatic.

'Is this the gun he was going to use, Ted?'

Beresford nodded.

Dawlish raised his eyebrows and looked at Mrs. Desmond.

'Do you happen to recognise it?' She stared at the gun and then at him, as if he had taken leave of his senses. Then, very slowly, began to examine it more closely.

'Why——' she began, stopped, then started again. 'I—I think

27

it was *Willy's*. I mean, Lieutenant Carr's! He—had one just like it.'

'I see,' said Dawlish heavily.

He turned and regarded Smythe, who appeared to have some difficulty in breathing.

'So you stole Carr's gun and you were going to shoot Mrs. Desmond with it. I wonder if——' he paused and reached out for the telephone again, dialling Scotland Yard and asking this time for Trivett's office. The sergeant to whom he spoke was able to answer his question offhand.

'Lieutenant Carr was killed by a .22 calibre bullet, sir.'

'Good, thanks,' said Dawlish, ringing off. 'A .22 calibre, and this is exactly that.' He began to smile, but there was no humour in his blue eyes, which were hard and cold as he looked at Smythe. 'You planned to make it look as if she had killed him and then committed suicide, that explains why you were fool enough to come here. First, you meant to find out what she knew about me, then to kill her and scotch the police investigation. Very neat indeed, if a little regardless of human life. All right, Smythe, you've a lot coming to you. Ted, did he hold the gun in a handkerchief?'

'Yes,' said Beresford, 'and I haven't fingered it.'

'Good man,' said Dawlish. 'Laura, have you ever held this gun?'

'Only—only in *play*. Did—did—did that kill Willy?' She shrank back a little too dramatically, and Dawlish, watching her closely, began to wonder if she were acting.

As soon as she had gone, he asked Beresford to take Smythe into the other room. Waiting until this had been done, and the door safely locked, he dialled his flat again. 'Felicity,' he said, 'watch Mrs. Desmond very closely, try to find out if she's putting on some kind of an act. Will you do that?'

'I'll try,' said Felicity promptly.

'That's fine. From a happily-married man to a happily-married woman, love and kisses! 'Bye!'

He quickly grew more sober. He had put on an act which he believed would lessen Smythe's power of resistance but needed a final touch, and it would be difficult to apply it here. On the other hand he could hardly march Smythe through the streets. Even if he did not try to escape, the man might attract attention with the object of getting into the hands of the police, rather than remain a prisoner of Dawlish's.

Suddenly he snapped his fingers with jubilation.

'Well take him out the back way, Ted! I've had an idea.'

'Let's hope it's a good one,' said Beresford, pessimistically.

'Good enough. Scout round the flat and see whether you can find a torch, will you?'

Smythe listened to all of this without speaking; from the way he looked from one to the other of them it seemed that he was beginning to weaken.

Before he opened the back door of the flat, Dawlish spoke thoughtfully.

'Ted, if he shouldn't come round, we'll have to get rid of him quickly.'

'Ah,' said Beresford, appearing to give the matter the right amount of cold-blooded attention. Smythe swallowed noisily and Dawlish looked away from him, frowning. 'Well, we can't back out now,' he said. 'Come on.' He opened the door and led the man down the iron steps which went into the narrow back garden of the block to the brick and concrete air-raid shelter at the back of the flats. A faint blue light with an 'S' sign showed near the entrance.

Inside, wooden benches ranged round the sides, against the bare walls, making the place look drear and bleak. It struck cold, also, and Smythe shivered.

Dawlish pushed him roughly to the far end of the shelter. His voice, when it came, was soft and expressionless.

'Have you any idea of what you're up against?'

'I—I've nothing to say,' muttered Smythe.

Dawlish said: 'Listen to me. You have killed, or helped to kill, at least three people. I am no respecter of persons and I am not a policeman. I mean to find out what you can tell me. You'll talk sooner or later, and you'll be well-advised to start before you get hurt.'

He put his hand into his pocket and drew it out inch by inch. It held a knife. Slowly he opened the blade. Smythe watched him with fascinated eyes, and began to mutter under his breath. Dawlish wondered whether the man would hold out long enough to thwart him. Threats of torture were right enough, but he could go no further. The question was whether Smythe's nerves would stand the strain, and he began to fear that they would. He seemed to take too long opening the knife, feeling the blade on his thumb, and then whetting it on the palm of his hand. All the time, Smythe watched him.

'All right out there, Ted?' Dawlish called.

'Half a mo,' said Beresford.

He went out, thus adding a few more precious seconds to the suspense, then came back and reported that everything was safe.

'Then here we go!' snapped Dawlish.

He shot out his left hand and grabbed Smythe's coat, pulling the man towards him; even in the poor light he could see the beads of perspiration on his forehead and upper-lip. There was a tense moment, when he thought he had failed: and then Smythe broke down.

'Don't do it!' he gasped, 'don't do it!'

'You've left it late,' Dawlish rasped. 'I'm not sure that you haven't left it too late. Did you come to kill Mrs. Desmond with Carr's gun?'

'Yes,' gasped Smythe, 'yes, but——'

He broke off, unable to speak for some seconds, but when he recovered enough he talked rapidly and comprehensively. Dawlish, knowing that there remained a great deal to learn, had the satisfaction of seeing the first crack in the enemy's defences.

CHAPTER SIX

DAWLISH SEES THE PRESS

BERESFORD went out of the shelter warily. Footsteps were approaching, heavy and deliberate, and he expected to meet a policeman. Instead he saw a warden's figure outlined against a faint light from a car, which passed and left the darkness more intense.

The warden had seen him, and Beresford went more than half-way to meet him in an endeavour to head him off.

'Hallo, hallo,' said Beresford. 'Still on duty around these parts, eh?'

The man's voice was suspicious. 'And might I ask what you are doing here?'

'Confound it, it's my own backyard,' said Beresford indignantly, 'or at least, the backyard of a friend.'

'No one has any business in a shelter unless——' began the warden, only to be interrupted.

Beresford immediately launched himself into a long-winded story which not only appeared to have no beginning but meandered on without hope of an end.

The warden's impatience was fast giving way to a fine fury when Dawlish and Smythe loomed out of the shelter.

'Hallo, there!' called Beresford. 'Any luck, Pat?'

'All O.K.' said Dawlish, who sounded pleased.

'There, you see?' said Beresford, turning to the warden. 'What did I tell you?' He clapped the bewildered man hastily on the back and sped after the other two. Smythe walked ahead. Dawlish had cowed him completely and he did not speak as they went up the iron steps.

Once in the sitting-room he dropped heavily into a chair, sitting forward, burying his face in his hands, a picture of such abject misery that Beresford felt a sneaking pity for him.

Dawlish's voice, however, was cold and hard. 'You know the position, don't you?'

'Yes,' muttered Smythe.

'If you don't do exactly as I tell you, the police will be informed at once,' continued Dawlish.

'If you do, when the whole show is finished you will have a chance of turning King's Evidence and saving your life. It's your only chance.' He poured out a drink and put it into Smythe's trembling fingers.

'Now go into that room and wait.'

Smythe lumbered towards it. As the door shut behind him, the grim expression on Dawlish's face altered and he grinned broadly.

'Doing fairly well?' asked Beresford.

'Thanks to you stalling the warden, we're doing fine. I know the name of the fat man and why they were on the lookout for me. Smythe says that he doesn't know what really lies behind it. He's an unofficial agent for Bloom——'

'Who's Bloom?'

'The fat man. I gather that he has been exerting some pressure and that Smythe is suffering for some indiscretions with his firm's accounts. I don't think Smythe amounts to very much.

31

These people are big, and Smythe isn't the type likely to be high in their counsels.'

'Hum,' said Beresford. 'Smythe had the nerve to come here to shoot Laura, didn't he? I mean, it wasn't bluff?'

'Oh, it wasn't bluff,' said Dawlish, 'he came to shoot her with Carr's gun all right. Her fingerprints were on it, or would have been pretty quickly. The idea was to make it look as if she had shot Carr and then, in a fit of remorse or fear, had killed herself. Smythe was prepared to do that. He didn't think there was any danger in it for himself, which was one of his major mistakes.' He lit a cigarette and went on: 'Apparently Bloom arranged for the murder of the two A.T.S. girls, although Smythe says that he doesn't know why. After the first, Bloom learned that I was taking a passing interest because Felicity was with that unit. Having heard of me'—Dawlish grinned—'he decided that I wanted watching. He got the idea that I saw something of what was really behind the murder. The lank-haired man saw Felicity near the scene of the second murder and heard her tell Sergeant Winneger to come for me. Lank Hair pelted off in pursuit. Bloom was waiting nearby and gave Lank Hair the job of following me, and according to Smythe, Bloom wasn't very pleased with him when he learned that he'd lost me. On the whole, we can't grumble.'

'Why not?' asked Beresford.

'Evidence of inferiority complex on the part of Bloom; he's decided that if I'm interested I might be dangerous. So, he's splitting his forces. Whatever he's doing must take up a lot of his time; remember he has the police to contend with. Taking it all in all, he isn't exactly having a holiday.'

'It rather looks as if we won't be either,' suggested Beresford. 'If he bumped off Carr and was prepared to put this fast one over on Laura Desmond, he isn't exactly a respecter of persons!'

Dawlish smiled. 'Oh, we're on his black list, but that doesn't greatly matter now that we know it.'

The room was silent for five minutes or more as he gazed abstractedly at the ceiling. Then, suddenly, he sat up abruptly.

'Got it!' he exclaimed.

'Got what?' asked Beresford.

'Too much to explain in a moment. Anyway, if Munk turns up again, have a row with him. Let Smythe listen-in to all of it, but don't let Munk know that Smythe is here.'

'Supposing he has a search-warrant with him?'

'He won't have,' said Dawlish. 'I'll be back in about an hour.'

He raised a hand in farewell and left the flat before Beresford really believed he was going. Not unused to the wayward habits of his friend, Beresford took the hurried departure philosophically, and bent his mind to the details of picking a quarrel with Munk.

There was no sound from the other room.

Dawlish hurried along the street until he saw a taxi approaching. He hailed it with relief.

'Fleet Street, Number 81A.'

Arriving at a large block of offices not far from the Law Courts, Dawlish alighted, pressed a note into the driver's hand with the injunction—'Wait twenty-five minutes, no longer,' and dived into the dark hall of 81A.

He began to climb the stairs to the second floor, on which were the offices of the Elmer News Agency. As an agency, the Elmer was not in the first class, but Dawlish knew that it had an unusual reputation. None of the big papers omitted to give the Elmer a hearing, because every now and again it brought off a remarkable scoop. The man responsible was the owner of the agency, an Anglo-American named Wright. Dawlish had once put an item of news in his way which had earned his promise of everlasting gratitude.

Without troubling to tap at the door, Dawlish went in.

The outer office was empty. Only the silent typewriters and brimming waste-paper baskets gave evidence of the end of a day's hard work.

Beneath a door leading from this room was a thin sliver of light.

Dawlish tapped, then pushed the door open without waiting for a response.

'Scram,' said a man, wearily.

Elmer Wright was lying on a camp bed. His sparse, grey hair was dishevelled as if he had run his hands many times through it. He looked at Dawlish with weary, blood-shot eyes.

Dawlish went in and closed the door.

'*Scram!*' repeated Wright, with slightly more emphasis.

Dawlish leaned against a large, overcrowded desk and regarded Wright patiently.

The journalist struggled to a sitting position. 'Who the heck are you, anyway?' He widened one eye, then whistled. 'Phe-ew! The great Dawlish, no other.'

'Nobody's as tired as he thinks he is,' said Dawlish smugly. 'That is, unless he's bone-lazy.'

'Who, me?' Wright swung one leg from the bed and took out a cigarette case. 'Bone-lazy?' He uttered a doleful 'ha-ha-ha!', lit up, and swung the other leg from the bed. 'Now look here, Dawlish, what the hell do you want?'

'Can you catch the last editions?' asked Dawlish.

'No,' said Wright emphatically. He got to his feet and walked slowly to the desk. 'What about?' he asked.

'The Kingston A.T.S. murder,' said Dawlish.

One of Wright's eyebrows shot up an inch higher than the other. 'Oh me, oh my!' he said. 'Listen, Dawlish, did you wake me up in the middle of the night to tell me the story of the murder of an At. Go away.'

'Can't you recognise a winner?'

'I can recognise the opposite number all right.' Wright gave a vast yawn. 'No news value on murder any more.'

'That's where you're wrong,' said Dawlish. 'Elmer, I want you to play up the Kingston murder as just another brutal crime. The louder that angle is played, the better. If you put it out yourself you can make some of the dailies take it up. You can also say that the police have decided to beat all records on this job and that an arrest is expected at any moment.'

'Gee!' exclaimed Wright, his eyes rounded in exaggerated amazement. 'Aren't you the world's most original phrase-framer!' He snorted. 'An arrest is expected at any moment! Now *where* have I heard that phrase before?'

'That's just the point,' said Dawlish patiently. 'An arrest *isn't* expected.'

Wright stared. 'I don't get you. I've been working hard all day. Better make it simple.'

Dawlish leaned forward. 'The girl murdered at Kingston was the second victim from the same camp. The man who is accused of the first murder couldn't have committed the second because he was in prison awaiting trial. There are circumstances suggesting that the murderer was the same in each case. I want you to do all you can to make sure that no one gets that angle. Play up the "clean up the country" line as hard as you can, and get every paper who'll run it to do the same. In other words, distract attention from the possibility that this time it's something different.'

'Oh,' said Wright. 'What's in it for me?'

'When the real story breaks—and there *is* one, I promise you —I'll see that you get the first news on it.'

'I hope you're right,' said Wright. 'Okay, I'll play.'

'Another thing,' went on Dawlish. 'You *might* have heard a rumour that I have been throwing my weight about and that the police don't like it.' He smiled. 'Will do?'

'*Now* you've got something,' said Wright, 'that's news value. Don't they love you any more?'

'Be vague, but make your meaning clear,' said Dawlish, 'I won't sue anyone for libel!'

Wright stared at him for some seconds, with a contemplative air, then grinned and bent his head to the desk.

When Dawlish reached Fleet Street again the taxi was waiting. He went straight back to Bethel Street, tipped the driver handsomely and went upstairs to find out if there had been any developments.

'There's one queer thing, Pat,' said Beresford. 'Smythe's been to sleep for an hour. He seemed to be having a nightmare. He kept muttering: "I didn't tell him that, I tell you, I didn't tell him that." I let him sleep on, in case I heard something more. But that was all.'

'Hum,' said Dawlish thoughtfully. 'I wonder if he did keep something back.' He considered the possibility for a moment, then put it at the back of his mind.

He was anxious to tell Beresford what he had done, and why. He wanted the general public as well as the man named Bloom to believe that the police considered the murder to be just one other in a series of sordid crimes, and that he, Dawlish, disagreed with them. That would afford Bloom some amusement; it would also encourage Bloom to think that he was at loggerheads with the police, a frame of mind that might make him careless.

'Why go to so much trouble to hoodwink Bloom?' asked Beresford with a certain disapproval. 'Must we make ourselves the Aunt Sallies?'

'Why, that's the whole idea,' said Dawlish triumphantly. 'We want to attract all the attention he can spare for us.'

'Munk hasn't shown up, I suppose?'

'No.'

'He wouldn't when we particularly want him to,' said Dawlish. 'I'll have a word with Trivett, I think. What's the time?'

'Not much past midnight,' said Beresford.

Trivett was not at the Yard and Dawlish, thinking that the policeman might be snatching a few hours' sleep, did not telephone him at his home. He replaced the receiver, regarded Beresford thoughtfully and then said that perhaps they had better have another go at Smythe.

'He's sleeping pretty soundly,' said Beresford.

'That's strange. That nervy type of chap seldom sleeps heavily,' said Dawlish, frowning. He stepped to the door of the spare room, flung it open and called 'Smythe!' in a loud voice.

The man lying on the bed did not stir.

'Smythe!' repeated Dawlish, in a louder voice and in some agitation. He stepped to the bed and shook the man vigorously. 'Smythe! Wake up!'

Still Smythe did not stir.

Dawlish took Smythe's right hand and felt his pulse. He looked into Beresford's face, and that ugly man's expression was set hard. The silence lengthened. Dawlish shook his head and then unbuttoned Smythe's waistcoat and felt his heart. There was no beating. To make doubly sure, he held a mirror in front of the man's lips, but it did not cloud over.

Beresford took out cigarettes, with slow deliberation. Dawlish took one and they lit up.

Dawlish said slowly. 'They must have drugged him before he started out. It's just as well we didn't lose any time, isn't it?'

'That's one point of view,' said Beresford. 'Another is, what are we going to do with him?'

CHAPTER SEVEN

AN INVITATION FROM MR. BLOSSOM

DAWLISH did not answer immediately. He led the way out of the room, locking the door behind them.

'Ted, we're going to be really unpopular,' he said.

'Again?' asked Beresford.

'It's my theory, right or wrong,' said Dawlish. 'I think that Mr. Bloom will like it if the police aren't well-disposed towards us. If Mr. Bloom also thinks that we've hidden this body without letting the police know where Smythe died, he will be tickled to death. Do you mind carrying Smythe downstairs and dumping him?'

'Now, come!' protested Beresford.

'Not on the pavement,' said Dawlish, judicially, 'but on the site of a bombed house or in an air-raid shelter or—— Well, choose where you like. We want to get him out of here.'

'I suppose you do know what you're talking about,' said Beresford. 'Now?'

'Right now,' said Dawlish.

'What are you going to do?'

'Telephone Trivett,' said Dawlish, 'or better still, go to see him. So long!'

He went out of the flat before Beresford, but he did not go far, making it appear that he was in a hurry, though, actually, he waited nearby. After five minutes Beresford entered the street; he was invisible except at a few yards' range, when it was possible to see that he was carrying Smythe over his shoulder. Presently Dawlish made out the figures of two men following Beresford. They did not go too near him, not even when Beresford chose the bombed-site on which to deposit the body, and they went off before Beresford had placed it to his liking.

When he was sure they had gone, Dawlish turned towards Chelsea. He was lucky enough to pick up a taxi which put him down at Withy Street.

It was here that Trivett lived.

Dawlish did not knock at the door at once; he wanted to marshal his thoughts so as to present a convincing case. The trouble was, that he could not really tell Trivett or anyone else what had prompted him to do exactly what he had done. The idea of confusing the mysterious Bloom was uppermost in his mind, and to that end he must try to get Trivett's co-operation.

At last he rang the bell.

Trivett himself opened the door. He was in a dressing-gown and his usually neat hair was awry.

'Who is it?' he demanded, and then his voice rose a shade. 'Well, I'm——'

'Hush!' said Dawlish reprovingly, 'it's too early in the morning for bad language!' He slipped into the hall, shading his eyes as the Superintendent switched on the light. 'I hope I didn't wake your wife up,' he added quietly.

'She's used to that,' said Trivett with the gloomy air of vicarious martyrdom. 'Like a cup of tea?'

'I could do with one,' said Dawlish. 'Shall we go and make it?'

'We!' exclaimed Trivett. 'A fat lot of help you'll be!'

As Trivett made the tea in a pleasant, modernised kitchen, Dawlish talked. He started off with the encounter with Smythe and all that had followed, and finished with the fact that Smythe's dead body was now reposing on the bombed-out site of a building not a hundred yards from Mrs. Desmond's flat. To all of this Trivett listened without batting an eye.

'And Beresford was watched and followed,' Dawlish said.

'Sugar?' asked Trivett, stirring placidly.

'No, thanks.'

'I suppose you do know what you're doing?' Trivett said, peering into the milk jug. 'Even you ought to know better than to cut capers like that with a dead body.'

'Oh, I do,' said Dawlish with a grin. 'Bill, it may not add up, but I think I've got under Bloom's skin. I want him to think that he can get under mine. I want to quarrel with you, in other words.'

Trivett gave a loud guffaw.

'One of your men finds Smythe's body and wants to know all about it,' said Dawlish, greatly encouraged. 'The papers take it up.' He sipped his tea, and when Trivett did not answer, went on: 'Unless Smythe lied to me, and I don't think that's likely, Bloom murdered Carr and arranged for the murder of Laura Desmond. Bloom was desperately anxious not to have Carr's murder connected with the murder of Mary Hill. To make sure that Smythe would not talk too freely, he dosed him with a delayed-action poison. It stopped me from learning one thing he kept back, although he told me a lot. As for the drug, one of the barbiturates would serve, if they knew how to use the doses and could judge the time they wanted Smythe alive.' Trivett still did not answer, and Dawlish went on: 'Bill, this is a big show. I don't know what it's about and I don't think you do——'

'I haven't a notion,' Trivett admitted.

'Well, we've got to find out. Will you try it my way?'

'It looks as if I shall have to,' said Trivett with a wry smile. 'But I do wish your plots weren't quite so devious, Pat.'

'But this one's simplicity itself!' cried Dawlish. 'Confound it, even at one o'clock in the morning you ought to be able to see that it will be an advantage if Bloom gets in touch with me. If he thinks you and I are quarrelling and that I've been warned off, and then adds to that the fact that I got the body out of the flat in a hurry, he'll make contact sooner or later.'

'I hope it's sooner,' said Trivett gloomily. 'All right, do it your way.'

'Now that's what I call good sense!' approved Dawlish.

'What about you and me? Do we cut each other in the street?' demanded Trivett, smiling.

'Oh, much worse than that,' said Dawlish. 'You have a policeman watching the flat all the time, but you tell him not to worry too much about losing me. Let Bloom find out for certain that I'm not *persona grata* any longer. It will fetch him, even if it's only out of sheer curiosity.'

Once Trivett had agreed to help in the subterfuge, Dawlish was not afraid of being let down. He left him a quarter of an hour later and arrived back in Bethel Street to find Beresford in an easy-chair; obviously he had been asleep, but had woken up at the first sound.

'Well?' he said at once.

'The trap's set,' said Dawlish, 'now we've got to wait for it to go off.'

'What are we?' demanded Beresford languidly. 'Rat poison or cheese?'

The remark seemed to please him so much that he chuckled intermittently for the next half-hour. There were two beds in the main room, and these they decided to occupy after locking and bolting the doors and making sure that the windows were fastened. There was no untoward incident during the night, and when they woke up within a few minutes of each other, just after eight o'clock, they felt ready for any new development.

There was little.

Trivett told Dawlish the results of his talk with Laura Desmond, while his inquiries in Kingston had brought several people who had been near Penrod's and seen something of what had happened.

The flat at Hillcrest Mansions, Putney, was visited and searched, but nothing very much was discovered there.

Elmer Wright had gone out of his way to use his influence with the Press; the situation Dawlish wanted to create was developing nicely. No one suggested that there was anything remarkable about the murder of Mary Hill, and two papers demanded a campaign for cleaning out the tiny minority which spoiled the good name of the Services.

It was all working out fairly satisfactorily.

Dawlish was not unduly depressed by the lack of immediate results.

The discovery of Smythe's body was reported in the Press and the inquest brought a verdict of wilful murder against some person or persons unknown. Nothing was said about the drug used, although Beresford, who went to the inquest, came back with a full report.

'Very dull,' he declared, stretching his long form in an easy-chair, 'and much medical detail. They did mention the name of the drug, but I don't think they were too sure of themselves. You were right when you suggested one of the barbiturates.'

'Let's not get lyrical,' intoned Tim Jeremy, a tall, thin young man lying back in another armchair. His voice was surprisingly deep and he possessed a facetious brand of humour which rarely misfired.

'How long do you expect us to be lolling about here, Pat? I wouldn't mind a day or two in the country. By Jove, for some curious reason, that reminds me!'

'What about?' asked Dawlish.

'Didn't Smythe have an appointment with a firm of biscuit manufacturers?'

'For tomorrow, yes,' said Dawlish, 'and I hope to keep it for him. The firm is Haling & Haling, Greenford. If I can't go, one of you had better hop along and find out what you can. It was probably a normal business appointment, anyhow.'

'Can't Trivett tell us for certain?' asked Beresford.

'I haven't asked him,' said Dawlish.

He did not add that he had not asked because he did not think that it mattered.

In that, the ignoring of what he considered to be unessential details, he was prepared to admit, he was sometimes wrong.

He was quite sure that he was not wrong about the interest which Bloom would take in him, and he questioned Beresford closely about the other members of the public at the inquest. He hoped to get some word of the lank-haired man, but none was forthcoming; if someone had been holding a watching brief for Bloom, Beresford had not been able to identify him.

They sat talking until nearly half-past six.

To disturb their serenity, the telephone rang.

Dawlish looked at it, just out of his reach. Jeremy frowned. Beresford opened one eye. At last, all three of them got up together.

Dawlish reached it first. 'Dawlish speaking.'

'Good evening, Major Dawlish,' said a man whose voice was unfamiliar, 'I am extremely glad that I have found you in.'

'Indeed,' said Dawlish evenly. 'Who is speaking?'

'I don't think you will know me,' said the speaker. 'My name is Blossom.'

'Blossom?' echoed Dawlish weakly.

'Perhaps you have heard of me.' The voice, mellow and cultured, appeared to have a touch of humour. 'Are you free this evening, Major Dawlish?'

'I'm afraid not,' said Dawlish gently.

'That is a pity,' said Blossom; the hint of laughter remained in his voice. 'I particularly wanted to see you, at Number 11 Pymm Place, Wimbledon. Oh, by the way, Captain Beresford is a close personal friend of yours, is he not?'

'What the devil are you talking about?' demanded Dawlish sharply. 'What have my friends to do with you?'

'I have a photograph of Captain Beresford carrying a some-what unusual bundle,' said the man who called himself Blossom. 'Don't misunderstand me, Major Dawlish! The photographs, negatives as well as prints, will be available if you care to break any prior engagements and come to Pymm Place this evening at seven-thirty. I did say Number 11, didn't I? *Good* evening, Major Dawlish!'

He rang off.

Beresford and Jeremy eyed the large man with eager interest. 'Mr. Blossom,' he murmured. 'A nice alternative to Bloom, don't you think? Ted, he photographed you when you were lugging Smythe out of the flat the other evening. He's no fool!'

'It was dark!' protested Beresford.

'Have you never heard of *infra dig*?' demanded Jeremy.

'Red,' corrected Dawlish absently. 'Number 11 Pymm Place, Wimbledon, at half-past seven tonight. Gentlemen, we are going to a party!'

'*All* of us?' demanded Beresford hopefully.

'Yes. You and Tim had better stay outside, but there'll be a party for all three of us before the night's over,' said Dawlish, and grinned more widely. 'Blossom or Bloom, what difference does it make?'

'Absolutely none,' said Jeremy gleefully.

He and Beresford were as gratified as Dawlish at the way things were shaping, and neither doubted that Mr. Bloom was going to experiment in blackmail. Whether he would see Dawlish in person was open to doubt. Dawlish did not greatly care; the move was what he had wanted, and now that it had come he believed that he could turn it to good advantage.

He telephoned Felicity to say that he would be out for the evening, then set Ted Beresford the task of discovering the exact position of Pymm Place. It was near the Common, a *cul-de-sac* containing only four large houses, he learned, two on either side of the road. The houses, comparatively modern, were surrounded by fair sized patches of ground. At the extreme end of the *cul-de-sac* there was a plot of land which was for sale.

'That's all useful stuff to know,' Dawlish said, 'and now we've just time for a sandwich, and then we'll get off.'

On their way to Wimbledon he mapped out what each of them was to do. Beresford was to approach the *cul-de-sac* across the plot of land, to be at hand without it being known that he was in support. Tim Jeremy was to wait outside, making himself noticeable so as to attract attention; by doing that, there was a reasonable chance that Beresford would not be seen.

This was as near a detailed plan of action as Dawlish was likely to evolve. For additional caution, Beresford got out of the train at Southfields, from where he was to make his way as best he could to the vacant plot.

At twenty-five past seven Dawlish and Jeremy turned into Pymm Place.

Partly hidden by hedges, Number 11 was discovered to be the second of the two on the right-hand side. Beyond it was common land, fringed by tall trees, now dark, almost forbidding shapes against an overcast sky. It was beginning to rain as they opened the gate.

Leaving Jeremy, as arranged, Dawlish walked briskly up a well-tended drive, past small, trim lawns and neat flower-beds ablaze with autumn flowers. On the lawn nearest the house was a hammock and a garden umbrella, and when Dawlish rang the bell he heard the bark of a pet dog.

'Most disarming,' murmured Dawlish.

The door was opened at once, and before Dawlish saw who opened it a fox terrier darted out, leaping high with excitement. Dawlish backed away, in surprise, as a pleasant feminine voice said:

'Down, Clam! Down!'

'Clam' made a frantic effort to lick Dawlish's hand, and then obeyed. A good looking, even beautiful, girl of perhaps twenty-five stood holding him.

'I'm so sorry,' she said, indicating the dog.

'Not at all,' murmured Dawlish, hiding a certain astonishment. Nothing less sinister could be imagined. 'I've an appointment with Mr. Blossom.'

The girl looked blank.

'Blossom?' she echoed. 'I'm afraid there's some mistake, no one of that name lives here.'

'Oh,' said Dawlish, stupidly. 'You're sure?'

She smiled. 'Oh, yes, I'm quite sure. I don't know of anyone named Blossom in Pymm Place, either—it's an unusual name, isn't it?'

'I suppose it is,' said Dawlish. 'Er—yes, most! I'm so sorry to have troubled you.' Utterly astounded, he turned away, followed by a disappointed yap from Clam and the puzzled gaze of the girl.

CHAPTER EIGHT

THE TRICKERY OF MR. BLOOM

DAWLISH stopped by the gate from where Tim Jeremy was unashamedly staring towards the house, and demanded irascibly:

'What do you think you're staring at?'

'Not what—who,' corrected Jeremy, beaming.

'I suppose it hadn't occurred to your stagnant mind that something has gone wrong,' said Dawlish with feeling. 'Don't stand there gaping at a closed door. Go and find Ted and tell him that we've been completely fooled.'

'Fooled,' echoed Jeremy. 'Oh, my hat, yes! Blossom! No Blossom?'

'Lord preserve me from the inanity of my friends,' said Dawlish righteously. It was unlikely that there was another Pymm Place in Wimbledon; possibly the man on the telephone had deliberately sent him to the wrong address. Neither Bloom nor Blossom were fools—if, in fact, they were two separate people, not the same man using horticultural aliases—and behind such a move there must be a powerful motive. Dawlish admitted that he was flummoxed. He lit a cigarette and watched Tim strolling across common land towards the road. A double-decker bus passed along the main road, a few hundred yards away, and was caught in a blaze of sunshine behind the dark banks of cloud. It had stopped raining, and birds were filling the air with an excited chattering.

Tim disappeared behind a clump of bushes. There he would find Beresford, Dawlish thought, and waited for a hail.

There was none forthcoming.

At last he saw Tim emerging from the trees. He raised a hand, beckoning Dawlish, then disappeared again. Dawlish, alert to danger, leapt over the fence and hurried across uneven grassland.

Tim was on his knees beside Beresford.

When Dawlish reached them, Beresford was opening his eyes. His lips were set tightly, as if he were in great pain.

'Nicely caught, Pat. Oooch!'

'What is it?' asked Dawlish.

'A trap,' said Tim, and he was not alluding to the way Beresford had been attacked, but pointing to a trap which gripped his right leg. Its ugly steel claws were bright and pointed, and there was blood on Beresford's sock and shoe.

Between them they prised it open, but it took all Dawlish's strength to hold it while Beresford's foot was withdrawn. He looked sombrely into Beresford's eyes.

'What else?' he asked.

'A clout over the head,' muttered Beresford.

By then Dawlish was taking off his friend's shoe, and Tim was examining the back of his head. The blow which had knocked him unconscious had broken the skin, and the hair was matted.

Dawlish straightened up.

'Tim, knock up that girl again and ask her if you can telephone for a doctor and a taxi, will you?'

He did not wait for an answer, but as Tim hurried off, he hoisted Beresford to his shoulders. It was a case of Ajax carrying Hercules, but Beresford was soon balanced fairly comfortably. Dawlish walked towards a gap in the fence, with Beresford over his shoulder in a fireman's hold. No one appeared to see them.

'How did it happen?' Dawlish asked.

'I walked straight into the damned thing,' Beresford said plaintively. 'I was hardly on the ground before someone came out of the trees and clouted me over the head. *Not* a nice evening,' he added.

'No. Did you see the man?'

'Not well enough to identify him again.'

'We appear to have been out-tricked by our Mr. Bloom,' said Dawlish.

He did not speak again until they reached the porch of Number 11. The girl was in the hall and Dawlish could hear Tim on the telephone. A middle-aged man in R.A.F. uniform was coming down the stairs.

'Daddy, there's been an accident and I've invited these gentlemen to use the morning-room until the doctor arrives.' The girl spoke quickly.

'Of course. An accident? H'm.' Her father did not speak again, but led the way to a room further along the hall. By the time Beresford was settled on a low divan, the girl came in with a bowl of water and a towel. She started to bathe the wound. Beresford looked at her dark head, bent near him and was sufficiently himself to wink at Dawlish.

The R.A.F. man introduced himself as Wing Commander Lampley. In the circumstances Dawlish felt that some kind of explanation was demanded. He told Lampley that he had been asked to come to the house to see a Mr. Blossom and that he was afraid that the accident had been deliberately engineered. He declared that he did not know why. Lampley took him to mean that he did not feel that he could say why.

'I see,' said the Wing Commander. 'It's most unfortunate.' The stiff phraseology gave some indication of his frame of mind. 'Do you propose to do anything about it?'

'How do you mean?' asked Dawlish.

'Er—well—the police——'

'Oh,' said Dawlish with a smile. 'That's all right, I don't think they will waste much sympathy on us!' He added laughingly that he had been rebuked by the police in the last day or two, and then gave his name. The firm lips of Wing Commander Lampley curved in a thoughtful smile.

'So you're Dawlish?'

'I'm afraid so,' said Dawlish. 'My wasted journey won't interest the police very much, I assure you. They'll say that I asked for trouble by butting in—and, you know, they wouldn't be far wrong!'

Lampley chuckled.

'Telephone them if you like,' Dawlish invited.

'Oh, I think——' began Lampley, only to be interrupted by his daughter.

'Daddy, that means——' she broke off, and Lampley said:

'Means what, Rene?'

Rene Lampley returned to Beresford's ankle, finished drying it with some cotton wool, bound a soft towel round it lightly and straightened up.

'It means that the men who caused this gave *our* address.'

'Yes. I——'

'Oh, come!' said Dawlish. 'It simply means that they knew Pymm Place and realised that it would be an ideal spot for their little exercise in tactics. There isn't the remotest connection otherwise, I assure you.'

'Of course there isn't,' said Rene quickly, 'but all the same, it's curious. Not many people know Pymm Place. It's right off the map, really, although it's so near the main road.'

'Anyone is likely to stumble across it by accident,' said Dawlish reassuringly, but it did not appear to reassure them.

From the moment the girl had put her thoughts into words, there had been a change in the attitude of both father and daughter. Dawlish sensed it, although he could not give it a name. There was, perhaps, a hint of apprehension and anxiety; it was no more than a hint, but it made him very thoughtful.

Then the doctor arrived.

He took one look at the ankle and declared that he would have to put in several stitches. He knew the Lampleys and apparently took it for granted that Rene had rendered first aid. She stood by while the minor operation was done. When it was finished, Beresford's forehead was damp, but there was a grin on his lips.

'All nicely sewn up,' he said. 'By George, I could do with a cup of tea!'

'I'll get one at once,' promised Rene.

The doctor asked whether they wanted him to arrange for an ambulance to take him home. Dawlish said that a taxi was on the way.

'That'll be all right, but don't let him put his foot to the ground or there'll be trouble. I don't think I need stay any longer, and I've several calls to make.'

The doctor went out, followed quickly by Lampley.

Beresford looked into Dawlish's eyes, obviously puzzled. Dawlish shrugged his shoulders and went to the door, which had been left ajar. Lampley and the doctor were engaged in a whispered conversation there. It was some time before the front door closed.

'Queer,' suggested Beresford.

'Remarkable,' agreed Dawlish. 'The case of the incurious doctor. Lampley put up a good act, didn't he? He pretended not to know what his daughter was talking about, although I think it sprang to his mind at once. There's trouble here and they're not as surprised as they'd like us to believe. The doctor is in their confidence, too. If he weren't he would have wanted to ask a lot of questions about the wound and how it was caused.'

'What do you make of it, Pat?'

'Nothing, yet, but Mr. Bloom goes up a notch or two.'

'You mean that he wanted us to meet the Lampleys?'

'What else could be behind it?' demanded Dawlish. 'What's more, they've a secret of some kind which they feel guilty about.'

'What are you going to do?'

'For the time being, nothing,' said Dawlish, 'but I hope they'll broach the subject. I wonder what's keeping Tim,' he added, glancing at his watch.

It was nearly nine o'clock.

A maid came in to draw the curtains and was followed by Rene Lampley with a tea-tray. Lampley did his best to appear affable, but when the taxi arrived there was little doubt of his relief.

Beresford was carried on an improvised stretcher to the taxi. A tip-up seat was lowered so that he could rest his leg, and he was comfortably installed. Tim stayed by the cab while Dawlish went back for a final word with the Lampleys. They met him in the hall.

'It's been remarkably good of you both,' Dawlish said. 'I don't know what we would have done without your help. Thank you so much.' He smiled as he shook hands.

Lampley assured him in an over-hearty manner that it had been no trouble at all. Rene was subdued, but the last thing Dawlish saw in the hall was the brightness of her smile; it was just a little too bright.

He walked thoughtfully along the garden path to the taxi. He and Tim stood on the pavement for a few seconds, and then Dawlish said:

'You'd better stay, to keep an eye on things, Tim.'

'I thought as much,' said Tim gloomily. 'Are they in it?'

'Blossom or Bloom's pitched them into it, and there's some kind of a flap going on there at the moment. I've half a mind to slip back and do some eavesdropping.' Dawlish hesitated, and then spoke more decisively. 'No, I won't, and we'll both leave here in the cab, anyhow. In you get!'

Dawlish waited until they were nearing Putney Hill, then tapped on the glass partition. The driver slid it open, and Dawlish said:

'Pull up for a moment, will you?'

The man obeyed.

'All right, Tim,' Dawlish said. 'Go back and keep your eyes wide open. I'll try to find someone to relieve you, but if no one arrives and nothing has happened by dawn, get back.'

'Am I looking for anything in particular?'

'For anything at all that strikes an odd note.'

It was characteristic of Tim to go back without demurring over the two apparently unnecessary miles of walking. He strode off and the taxi moved away from the kerb. The driver was going cautiously and Beresford assured Dawlish that he was comfortable.

'In body, if not in mind,' he added. 'I liked the Lampleys.'

'Yes. They're likeable folk. Blossom or Bloom sent us there and it could only be because he wants to arouse our interest in them. The plot is certainly thickening. We know that Bloom had a man nearby because of the fellow who clouted you. There might have been others. The doctor's mixed up in something queer, too, he was far too easily satisfied. Lampley didn't press the point about the police, either, and tried to pretend that it was because he sympathised with me. He didn't wholly succeed. Deep waters, Ted!'

'And I'm a non-swimmer,' said Beresford, with a touch of bitterness. 'Blast them and their man-traps!'

'You're lucky that your ankle isn't broken,' said Dawlish. 'In any case, this may be a long-term business and you might be in at the kill.'

'Don't blether,' said Beresford crossly. 'I'm laid up for a fortnight at least. You'll have to try to get hold of someone else, you and Tim won't be enough for this.'

Little more was said on the journey.

They went to Dawlish's flat, and again Dawlish carried Beresford in a fireman's hold. As he heard Felicity coming to open the door, he called out to reassure her that things looked worse than they were. She assumed that he had been hurt, and she looked almost indecently relieved when she saw that Beresford was the victim. Before she could ask questions, Dawlish kissed her on the tip of her nose, dumped Beresford on a couch and said that he would be back within half an hour.

Felicity stared at the closed door, then turned and looked at Beresford with an inquisitive gleam in her eyes. He gave her a résumé of what had happened, and swore that he did not know where Dawlish had gone.

Dawlish had, in fact, decided on waiting until morning before trying to get someone else to help, but at the last minute had changed his mind. That was simply because he had seen Felicity. He did not feel happy about leaving her alone at the flat, or even with the company of Laura Desmond. So he had decided that he must get reinforcements quickly.

The branch of Intelligence for which he worked was not remarkable for its brawny young men; he, Tim and Ted had, for a while, comprised most of the strong-arm staff. Recently, however, there had been two additions, men who shared a flat nearby and whom, he knew, were off duty the next day. He hoped to be able to press them into service, and to arrange for their official help from Colonel Whitehead.

The name of one of the men was Creem, and of the other, Napier. Creem was the older of the two. Stocky and powerful, dark-haired and quick-witted, he was a decisive individual. Napier was a tall, willowy man who managed to create the impression of perpetual lassitude. This deception was aided by his wavy, corn-coloured hair and his large blue eyes, which always seemed half-closed.

They showed no umbrage at being woken up just after twelve o'clock, and immediately assumed that Dawlish had come on official business. He told them the truth, without wasting time, and asked for their help at least until the following day. He had not finished speaking before Creem was stripping off pale blue pyjamas and Napier was saying: 'By George, count us in!'

Dawlish sent them both to Wimbledon with a message to Tim advising him to get some sleep, then returned to the flat. There he helped Beresford to bed, and made his peace with Felicity.

His last waking thoughts were of the Lampleys.

He slept so heavily that he knew nothing until Felicity brought him an early cup of tea. Ted was asleep, she said, and it seemed a pity to wake him. She admitted that she was relieved that Laura Desmond would not be worrying her that day; relatives of Laura's were coming to see her, and her time would be fully occupied.

'But *mine* won't,' said Felicity.

'Yours will,' said Dawlish sternly. 'You're nursing Ted.'

'No, Pat, he doesn't need nursing, and the quicker this business is over the better it will be for all of us. There must be something I can do.'

Dawlish sipped his tea.

'At the moment there's absolutely nothing. We're all of us

rather waiting on this Bloom individual, you know, and so far he's managed to side-track us very neatly. I wonder if he did photograph Ted and the body?' he added thoughtfully.

'Now you're trying to side-track me,' said Felicity.

'Not entirely. Bloom is still dictating the pace. Though he's started to nibble at the bait.' Dawlish looked at the clock, gave an exclamation of astonishment and leapt out of bed.

By the time he had bathed, shaved and breakfasted, Beresford was awake. His colour was high and his eyes overbright; neither Dawlish nor Felicity was surprised when the doctor told them that he was running a temperature.

'I don't like the look of the ankle too much, either,' he added decisively. 'I think it would be wiser to have him under observation.'

'A nursing-home?' asked Felicity.

'I think hospital would be better. Exactly what caused the wound, Dawlish?'

'He stepped into a trap.'

'A trap! It must have been man-size! I'll arrange for an ambulance to be sent. Shall I tell him or will you?'

'No, I'll manage him,' said Dawlish.

It was a development which Dawlish had not expected. They waited without speaking until the ambulance came and Beresford was taken off to the Bray Street Hospital. When he had gone, Dawlish and Felicity sat opposite each other in silence.

Felicity broke it.

'Pat——' she began, and then stopped.

'I know,' said Dawlish. 'Smythe died when there seemed to be nothing the matter with him, he was drugged before we got him here. No ordinary wound should turn like that. Possibility: that the teeth of that trap were infected.'

He stood up, restlessly, and approached the window. 'I wish I had even a faint idea of what it's all about. Bloom and Blossom are nebulous individuals, the lank-haired customer has disappeared, and we've only the biscuit manufacturers and the odd tattoo mark to give us any guide at all. I'd better see the biscuit people, I suppose.'

'Well, you can get there and back in a couple of hours,' said Felicity hopefully.

'And I will!' said Dawlish.

He waited until Tim arrived, fresh from a good sleep. Nothing had happened at Wimbledon the previous night, and he had promised to relieve Creem and Napier during the morning.

'Do that,' said Dawlish. 'I mustn't forget to have a word with Whitehead, either, we shall probably need them after today.' In the train to Greenford he scanned the papers and found that Elmer Wright's influence was still making itself felt in one or two of them. There was a write-up about Penrose, the man accused of the first A.T.S. murder, in one paper, with a photograph of the man.

He looked a pleasant enough fellow, about twenty-six or seven.

'We'll have to get him out of the jam he's in, poor chap,' Dawlish mused, and then he left the papers on his seat and got out of the train.

He could not get a taxi at the station and had to walk a mile and a half before he reached the biscuit factory. Haling & Haling, Limited, were in temporary premises as their main factory in North London had been bombed out. This one was a jerry-built place, near another building which looked deserted.

There was a different impression inside, however; the offices were modern, and a business-like girl received Dawlish with unusual promptitude. Dawlish was well-primed. He had come to see Mr. Charles Haling, in place of Mr. Bertram Smythe, and he had an appointment for twelve o'clock. The name he gave was 'Hall'.

The girl was gone only a few minutes before she returnd to say that Mr. Haling would see Mr. Hall at once. Dawlish followed her up a flight of narrow stairs, and then tapped on a door on which was written: '*Mr. Charles Haling, Director*'.

Dawlish's guide opened the door, standing aside for him to enter. Dawlish stepped through—then pulled up short, staring in surprise as great as that of the girl facing him.

She was Rene Lampley.

CHAPTER NINE

THE PUZZLEMENT OF MR. HALING

DAWLISH and Rene Lampley were alone in the small office. The girl stood staring at him, the colour drained from her cheeks.

'What——' she began, and then stopped.

'Mr. Hall, to see Mr. Haling,' Dawlish said ironically.

'You——' she began.

What she would have said, Dawlish had no idea, for at that moment a door opened and a man appeared.

He looked at Dawlish. 'Mr. Hall?'

'That's right,' said Dawlish.

Rene kept her face averted, and Haling did not appear to notice that there was anything the matter. He ushered Dawlish into his private office, a large, low-ceilinged room, more expensively furnished than Dawlish had expected.

Charles Haling looked a well-dressed, prosperous business man. The alertness of his expression was the most noticeable thing about him; he would miss very little, Dawlish thought.

'Sit down, Mr. Hall,' he said in a voice that gave nothing away. 'I am glad you have called. Mr. Smythe's letter puzzled me, and the events which followed it have puzzled me even more.'

'Indeed,' said Dawlish.

'You will hardly find that surprising,' said Haling. 'Now, sir, what can I do for you?'

Dawlish said: 'To what events were you referring, Mr. Haling?'

'Now, sir!' Haling was brisk. 'I read the papers and I read of the discovery of the body of a man named Smythe. I have never seen him, so that the photograph which appeared in the papers gave me no help. On the other hand the address in the papers was the address from which he wrote to me. Are you a friend of his?'

'No,' said Dawlish.

'Then I take it that you are a business associate. I hope you can explain his curiously-worded letter.'

'As a matter of fact, I haven't seen it,' said Dawlish, truthfully. 'Is it handy?'

Haling frowned, then opened a folder on the desk, selected an open sheet of paper and handed it to Dawlish.

Dear Sir [Dawlish read],

You will not know me, but it is essential for your own peace of mind and for the continued prosperity of your business for you to see me on Thursday next, at twelve noon. I do not think you will be in any doubt as to my meaning. I look forward to your confirmation of the appointment.

Yours faithfully
Bertram C. Smythe.

Dawlish read it twice then returned it, looking bewilderedly into Haling's eyes. Yet he did not escape the impression that Haling was wary as well as puzzled.

'Well?' asked Haling.

'I suppose you knew what he was talking about,' said Dawlish, playing for time.

'I did not!' Haling spoke sharply. 'Nor do I know now. I hope that you will be able to explain. I confirmed the appointment because I intended to find out what he implied, and to send him about his business. Are you telling me that you do not know what Smythe meant?'

'Yes. I——'

'Then be good enough to tell me what you mean by coming here on the strength of his appointment!' snapped Haling.

The man was used to having his own way. There was no bluff nor bluster about him, just a sharp, decisive manner born of authority.

'In what paper did you read of the murder of Smythe?' asked Dawlish, quietly.

'Since you are interested, *The Morning Cry*, Mr. Hall.'

'Not Hall,' said Dawlish. 'Major Dawlish.'

The only sign that Haling gave of his reaction to this piece of news was the slight narrowing of his eyes.

He recovered quickly.

'Major Dawlish!' he echoed. 'Well, Major Dawlish, I have been very patient with you. You have come here using a false name, presumably with the intention of trying to get information. I must ask you to explain yourself.'

Dawlish said easily. 'It's quite simple, really. I think the two murders are connected. True, the police don't agree with me. But——'

'Do I understand that you are investigating the murder of Smythe, and that of the A.T.S. girl, purely as a private individual?'

'If you put it like that, yes,' said Dawlish.

'I have no more to say to you,' said Haling decisively. 'I am at the disposal of the police, if they should want to ask me questions, although there is little I can tell them. Smythe's letter was a complete mystery to me. So was the purpose of his visit. The police——' Haling paused, and then leaned forward a little. 'Major Dawlish, you are a very brazen young man!'

'Am I?' asked Dawlish.

'You admit that you are not connected with the authorities, you have the impertinence to come here to question me, and at the same time you tell me that you knew Smythe before he was killed.'

'Oh? How's that?' demanded Dawlish.

'How else could you have known about this appointment?' demanded Haling. His voice hardened. 'I think I must ask you to explain your knowledge to the police, Major Dawlish.' His hand hovered about the telephone. 'That is unless you can give me a very good reason why I should not do so.'

'Ah!' thought Dawlish. 'There's a chink in his armour!'

He returned Haling's gaze steadily. The plump, well-manicured hand rested on the telephone receiver, but did not lift it.

Dawlish said:

'I wonder if Miss Lampley is a sufficient reason, Mr. Haling?'

There followed a moment of strained silence.

At last, Haling said very softly: 'Major Dawlish, I have this to say to you. I shall tell the police of your visit just as soon as it is convenient. You have no right here and no grounds for mentioning my secretary in this connection. But for the risk of causing her unpleasantness, I should send for the police immediately.'

'Would you?' asked Dawlish. 'I wonder.'

There was no point in forcing an issue now. He had learned a little, and he had succeeded in getting under Haling's skin. There was trouble with the Lampleys, and Haling was not unaware of it. Later he would have to find out more, but for the time being it would be better to let them worry over what he might do. He stood up.

'I think that's about all,' he said easily.

Haling made no effort to stop him.

The outer office was empty and he saw no sign of Rene Lampley. No one was in the hall. He went out into the yard and strolled towards the second building. A workman rolling some barrels volunteered the information that it was a 'shadow factory'—ready to be put into operation if the main building was damaged, or for production as soon as more raw materials became available.

Dawlish wandered round, trying to find a short cut and also to find out if he were watched. No one seemed interested in him. When he reached the road, he was still on the alert, expecting Bloom to have a man near even if Haling did not send one to follow him. He was acutely conscious of the influence of Bloom, even though he had never seen him. In his mind he conjured up visions of a massive man with something of Haling's decisive manner.

A train was due at half-past one, and he had little more than ten minutes to wait. He strolled up towards the end of the platform. Suddenly he stopped.

Rene Lampley was waiting for him, smiling.

Dawlish liked her for the brave smile. She was clearly afraid and on edge.

'Why, hallo!' he said. 'Are you catching my train?'

'Yes,' she said. 'Major Dawlish, I want to talk to you and I don't want to be overheard.'

'Then let's go further up the platform,' suggested Dawlish. 'There are only half a dozen people waiting. We'll be private enough.' He took her arm and led her forward.

'Well, now,' he said, 'what is it all about, Miss Lampley? I'm anxious to help; I think you know that.'

'I wonder if you are,' she said.

She gave him a quick, hopeful smile.

'I *hope* you are! I tried to persuade my father to tell you something about it last night, but he wouldn't. I don't suppose he will like it, nor will Haling, for that matter, but—well, I'm going to take the chance.'

'Splendid!' said Dawlish.

'The trouble is that I hardly know where to start,' said Rene with a catch in her voice. 'It's all so confusing and complicated. It really begins, I suppose, with Penrose.'

'*Penrose!*'

He could not help himself; the name sprang from his lips. It gave away the fact that he had not expected her to know Penrose, *who was the man waiting for trial for the murder of Clara Stuart*! She looked at him with startled surprise, and also with some alarm.

'Surely you knew——' she began, and then broke off. She turned round, as if she wanted to get away, already repenting her confidence.

The silence between them was broken by the ringing of a bell signalling the approaching train.

'Why on earth did you come here, if you didn't know?' she demanded at last.

'I knew that there was a possible connection between the murder of Smythe and Haling & Haling,' Dawlish said. 'Look here, Miss Lampley, I'm not an enemy and I'm not trying to trick you. You saw what happened to a friend of mine last night. I think whoever did it is a murderer, and I want to make sure. I think he is responsible for the murder of Clara Stuart, the crime of which Penrose is accused. Does that make sense?'

'Are you telling the truth?' she asked.

'Of course I am! How do you know Penrose?'

She said: 'I don't know him personally. He was on the staff at the firm, on the advertising section.' She hesitated, marshalling her thoughts. 'He was called up before I went to the office to help out with the staff shortage. I had heard of him but never met him personally. You believe that, don't you?'

'Why shouldn't I?' asked Dawlish.

She ignored the comment.

'Penrose was popular and clever and well-liked,' she said. 'My father thought a great deal of him——'

'Can we stop for a moment to get one thing straight?' asked Dawlish with a smile. The bell clanged again and in the distance there was the slight rumble of the approaching train. 'What is your father's connection with the firm of Haling & Haling?'

'He's the senior partner,' she said, as if astonished by his ignorance.

'Oh!'

'He was in the R.F.C. in the last war and immediately volunteered in this one,' said Rene, 'so he hasn't much time for the business. Charles and George Haling are the junior partners —sons of the original Haling.' The rumble of the train grew louder. 'When several of the staff were called up, Charles Haling wanted a private and confidential secretary. I took the job. As a matter of fact, I wanted to join the Wrens,' she said with a grimace, 'but father persuaded me against it, and I've been there for three years now. Penrose left just before I joined.'

'I see,' said Dawlish.

'He was in hospital on and off for two years overseas, before coming back here,' said Rene. 'We wanted him back on the staff and tried to get his release from the army, but they said he was capable of doing a job in England, although actually he's not been fit enough to do much. Why *am* I talking like this?' she added, distractedly. 'I can't think clearly! I suppose the truth is that the trouble *does* start with Penrose. That is, it wasn't until he was arrested for murder that we had any serious bother. And now here's the train!'

The train was, indeed, drawing into the station, and the platform was fairly crowded. It was no more than a hundred yards away when a thin, lank-haired man ran towards Dawlish and Rene.

Dawlish swung round but he was too late to fend the man off, and too late to save himself from a blow which sent him staggering to the edge of the platform. He felt Rene's hand touch his, but she could not get a grip; his weight would have dragged her with him, in any case. Someone screamed further along the platform. The train came nearer and Dawlish tried to regain his balance, first on one foot and then the other, while the man with lank hair raced on down the platform, scaling the railings which divided the railway track from the road.

CHAPTER TEN

LIVE WIRE

DAWLISH knew that he was going to fall.

The train was the lesser threat; the nightmare was the live wire. He was falling forward, with his right leg off the platform. The train was screeching, as if the driver had seen the emergency and was applying the brakes. The live wire was near the platform; the actual railway line was next to it.

He brought his left leg off the platform and jumped.

He landed between the tracks but did not regain his balance quickly enough to save himself from pitching forward. In his ears were the screams of women and the braking of the train, which he knew was now dangerously close. He stumbled, falling as straight between the lines as he could.

The fall jolted him, but he remained conscious.

He lay still, not quite sure whether he was safe or not, his head reeling. He heard confused shouting, and thought that someone jumped down from the far platform. A moment later a man bent over him and spoke in a rough, anxious voice.

'Okay, sir, okay, the current's off!'

Dawlish drew in his breath.

The man helped him to his feet. The screaming woman's voice reached a new high pitch and Dawlish wished irritably that she would stop. He was still unsteady, his face ashen pale. He limped painfully towards the edge of the track, and it took the porter who had come to his aid and two others to get him up to the platform. They half led, half carried, him to the nearest seat, to which he sank, trembling from head to foot.

Several people came hurriedly including Rene Lampley and a thick-set man who declared himself a doctor. A passenger offered a flask of brandy and after a few sips Dawlish began to feel something of a fool. The train moved out of the station and he could see the curious faces of passengers pressed against the windows.

The faces of the people near him were less steady. Rene's seemed to go round and round; one moment close to him, the next, a long way off.

Someone brought him a cup of tea, and when he had finished

it the colour was back in his cheeks and he was able to speak reassuringly.

At last, the inevitable policeman arrived.

Dawlish declared flatly that he had no idea why he had been attacked and that he had never seen the man who had pushed him before. Was the man still at large?

'He won't be, for long,' said the constable, 'several people saw him, sir.'

He was an understanding man, questioned others more closely than Dawlish himself, and then checked over the big man's name and address before saying that there was nothing that need detain him now. Gratefully, Dawlish got to his feet. He walked steadily for a few yards, Rene was by his side. Finally one of the porters said that there was an empty taxi outside, and suggested that Dawlish might prefer to go home by car.

Dawlish thankfully agreed, and they reached the flat a little after three o'clock. Dawlish, who had discovered that his clothes were torn and that he had a scratch on his forehead and another on his right cheek, went into the bathroom for a wash, after introducing Rene and Felicity; Tim needed no introduction, and after a short interval left the two women together, and joined Dawlish in the bathroom.

'Now what?' he asked.

'Leave questions for a minute,' said Dawlish. 'Have you sent a message to Creem and Napier?'

'I've done better,' said Tim. 'I had a word with Whitehead, who agreed that they could lend us a hand, unless anything crops up at the office. Napier's at Wimbledon by himself and Creem is having a nap. He'll go back to relieve Napier about six o'clock. How does that sound?'

'Good work,' said Dawlish, 'I couldn't have done better myself!'

He moved his shoulder gingerly, dabbed iodine on the scratches and then rejoined the others. He still felt unsteady, and he hoped that no sudden emergency would present itself.

'Well, where do we go from here?' Dawlish asked.

'I was just telling your wife——' began Rene, and ran over the details very briefly. When she came to the point where their conversation had finished at Greenford, her colour had heightened. 'That's all, except——'

'The real trouble,' said Dawlish.

'Yes. I wonder if you can understand what I'm going to talk about?'

'It's possible,' said Dawlish dryly.

'The difficulties began when the firm offered to support Penrose,' said Rene unhappily. 'As I've told you, I've never met him, but Mr. Haling and others on the staff were quite sure that he was innocent. Haling went to see him and came back even more convinced than ever. So the firm decided to pay for his defence.'

'This is getting interesting,' said Dawlish, and remembered that Trivett had told him that Penrose's employers were looking after his defence. Had he shown the letter to Trivett, the Superintendent would have known that Haling & Haling were indirectly concerned. He thought ruefully, too, that this was an occasion when his carelessness about detail had failed him; he had not asked Trivett for the name of the accused man's employers.

'Almost from the time of Penrose's arrest, things went wrong,' said Rene helplessly. 'There was a fire at the factory—not a serious one, but enough to delay production and to destroy some raw materials. And then a boiler exploded. Both seemed accidental, and yet there was no way in which we could explain them. The insurance company weren't too happy, and talked of sabotage, but Haling & Haling isn't a large enough food manufacturing firm to make that worth while.'

'You'd think not,' admitted Dawlish.

'There were other things,' said Rene. 'We had a trusted accountant and cashier, who'd been with the firm for about thirty years. A serious shortage was found in his accounts. He swears that he knows nothing about it, but some of the money was found in his desk. Of course, we had to suspend him, although we haven't yet reported it to the police. If it were just that he had slipped up, I don't think we would, but if there's something else behind it, that's a different matter.'

'It certainly is,' said Dawlish.

Obviously there was something she had not yet broached. So far she had explained enough to make it clear why she and her father and the Halings had grounds for being worried, but there was evidence that they were all reluctant to talk about it. She herself had apparently defied Lampley by seeing Dawlish; that was not solely because of the trouble at the factory.

'At one time things were going quite smoothly,' said Rene, 'and then everything began to go wrong at the same time. And—there's something else.'

No one prompted the girl.

'It will sound fantastic,' Rene went on helplessly, 'and yet—well, we *don't* know!'

Still no one prompted her.

'I'm sure that George Haling knows something about it, but it will be hard to convince the police of that,' said Rene. 'I think he was wrong not to report it from the moment he first heard of it. Now it's too late, and it will be difficult to explain why he kept silent.' She did not seem to realise how exasperating she was being; she appeared bewildered, obviously, and she hated broaching the crux of her story. Dawlish wondered if it would be an anti-climax as far as he was concerned, but what she said next startled him. 'We have a fleet of fifteen delivery vans,' she said abruptly. 'Most of them used only by day. About six weeks ago, just after the Penrose affair, we discovered that eight or nine of them were being taken out, secretly, by night.'

'Did you stop it immediately?'

'We tried to,' said Rene, 'but it didn't seem to matter what man we had watching, two or three of the vans always went out. The watchmen just *couldn't* keep awake!' She looked at Dawlish intently. 'I know we ought to have gone to the police, and I know we ought to have found some way of stopping it, but—well, *we* wanted to find out what it was about, and we tried. We failed,' she added, and she looked worried, even frightened. 'We don't know what the vans were used for, we only know that they were taken from the garage and brought back before the factory opened next morning. There's been no trouble during the last month, yet we're always on edge about it.'

'If you found it out six weeks ago and it hasn't been happening for a month, you didn't really fail to stop it,' said Dawlish. 'What makes you say that you did?'

'I didn't. I said we'd failed to find out why it was being done.'

'So you did,' said Dawlish. 'In the fortnight that you were having the garage watched, the vans still went out sometimes, and the man watching fell asleep. Is that it?'

'Yes. Even *I* did!'

'Did you, by George!' exclaimed Dawlish.

'Yes. And Charles Haling. It—it rather stung us,' went on Rene. 'We felt that we were being made fools of. When my father came home on leave, just after we'd discovered what was happening, he spent a night watching. That night someone came but found Daddy awake. There was a bit of a struggle, but the man got away. On other nights the watcher would wake up after falling asleep for several hours. The vans had been out but were back again. You—you see what a difficulty it is.'

Dawlish grinned, unexpectedly.

'There's no law against it. The vans were the company's even if they were being unlawfully used. It is usual to notify the police, but I can't see that it's anything serious to have a stab at finding out yourself.'

'Do you mean that?' Rene looked more eager.

'Of course I do,' said Dawlish. 'Where you would come unstuck is if you knew that the vans were being used for something criminal and still didn't report it. You don't know why they've been used?'

'Of course not!'

'Then what's all the fuss about?' asked Dawlish.

He did not think that she had told him the whole truth, and he wondered if she was afraid that someone did know why the vans went out by night. She might suspect her father or Haling of knowing, and be reluctant to voice her suspicions, but at heart she knew that Dawlish would realise that they existed. It was a curiously unsatisfactory climax.

Dawlish said: 'It looks as if there's been a lot of anxiety over a simple enough thing, Miss Lampley. I——'

Rene said: 'You don't really believe that!'

She stood up as she spoke.

'I shouldn't have expected to satisfy you so easily. The trouble is, it's *nearly* the whole truth. I can't tell you any more, except——' she broke off.

Dawlish said, quietly: 'All right, let's have it straight. You think that your father or Haling know why the vans are being used, don't you? And you're afraid that it's for an illegal purpose? It probably is,' he added, 'and one or both of them might be involved in it. That's what's frightening you, isn't it?'

'I suppose it is,' she said.

Dawlish smiled, looking into eyes as blue as his own.

'Look here, Rene, we've got to tackle this business on a sound basis. When I called on you last night you weren't looking over your shoulder or scared of a sudden manifestation of the police. What brought about the change?'

'I don't know,' she said quickly. 'After all, nothing much has happened for over three weeks. Even the last trouble at the factory was three weeks ago. One forgets.'

'Not altogether,' said Dawlish. 'One can put unpleasant thoughts aside for a while, but they have a way of creeping back. Until I came last night, it was one of your successful "lets-forget-it-I-must-be-exaggerating" spells, was it?'

He made her smile.

'Yes and no,' she said. 'I *had* been seriously worried because I thought my father was. He went back to his station for a fortnight and only came home again last evening. He seemed perfectly happy and we talked about it quite freely. I felt quite sure that he knew nothing about whatever was happening and so—well, I was pleased with life!'

Probably the same high spirits had prevailed until the dark thought had occurred to her that someone had deliberately sent Dawlish to the house. From that moment onwards her fears had returned, he thought, and she had been a different woman.

It was all very natural, Dawlish decided; but it left her father's attitude unexplained.

'And that's all?' asked Dawlish.

'You can't expect much more,' said Rene.

'Dickens had nothing on me for great expectations!' declared Dawlish.

Rene asked: 'What happened between you and Charles Haling?'

Dawlish told her, and Felicity and Tim listened with equal interest. It grew obvious that Haling had connected the mystery of the company's vans with the murder of Smythe. It was equally clear that he was nervous, although the fact that he had evaded going to the police might explain that. On the other hand, he might know more than he pretended. When Dawlish finished, Felicity said quickly:

'What happened to you, Pat?'

'Lank Hair tried to push me in front of a train.'

'Tried!' exclaimed Rene. 'I've never been so horrified!'

'Oh, he was fairly proficient,' admitted Dawlish. 'These people know their job. Forgetting that for the moment'—he made a grimace at Felicity—'what about this falling asleep while on guard business? Did you go away from the factory and return after dark?'

'No. We had dinner at the canteen.'

'Did you have anything to eat or drink after dinner?'

'Usually we had some tea or milk, last thing,' said Rene.

'That probably explains the attack of sleepiness,' said Dawlish, 'you were given a sure-to-act sedative in your drink. Who made the drinks?'

'The night-watchman,' said Rene.

'Always the same man?'

'Yes,' she said, her eyes widening. 'Yes, of course! Why on earth haven't I thought of that before?'

Dawlish was prepared to admit that she had not thought of it now, but he did not believe that neither Haling nor her father had missed such an obvious explanation. It grew clear that neither of them had really confided in her. He did not think it wise to take her on trust yet, but he was inclined to believe that she had told the truth as far as she knew it. He had one shot in his locker, and he fired it then.

'That's good. Now—do you know your doctor well?'

'Dr. Mordaunt? Oh, yes, he's a family friend,' Rene said, 'and the official factory doctor. Why——?'

She broke off, presumably because she had been seized with another unpleasant thought. She looked at him with increasing anxiety, and then suddenly looked away.

'Be wholly frank,' said Dawlish earnestly. 'Nothing else will get us anywhere.'

She said: 'But he's known me all my life!' No one else spoke, and she went on reluctantly: 'He holds shares in the business——' she faltered again.

'We must have it all if we're to clear it up,' Dawlish said reasonably.

'I've never really thought of this before,' Rene said, 'but last night my father and Dr. Mordaunt had a talk together, I noticed them at the door. Now you've made me think of that, I recall other whispered consultations which stopped as soon as I got within earshot.' She had lost much of her colour, and looked distraught. 'What *am* I doing!' she exclaimed.

'You know that this might be connected with Smythe's murder, don't you?'

'In what way?'

'Whoever killed Smythe had a motive,' said Dawlish. 'Smythe wrote a letter which the police would think threatening. They might also think that Haling knew what Smythe was talking about in the letter, and killed him to prevent any disclosures.'

'Oh,' she said helplessly. 'It's getting worse!'

Certainly it was not getting any clearer, except for the indubitable fact that Haling & Haling Limited was in some way connected with the murder of Smythe and the two girls, and with all that had gone before. Had Dawlish come upon this in a more straightforward way, he would have put Haling & Haling high on the list of suspects, but he could not get away from one fact: Bloom or Blossom had sent him to 11 Pymm Place, and had therefore hoped that he would find this out.

There was another point upon which the police would concentrate; immediately after his interview with Haling there had been an attempt on Dawlish's life. It was not unreasonable to think that Haling, thoroughly alarmed, might have sent Lank Hair to do away with him. He wondered if Rene had thought of that, and realised that she had, for she said slowly:

'Major Dawlish, I'm quite sure that Haling didn't know anything about the attack on you.'

'I admire your loyalty,' said Dawlish gently, 'but, you know, you can't be sure.'

'It's fantastic even to think that he did!' she exclaimed.

Yet she was obviously afraid that Haling knew about Lank Hair and of all that had happened, and Dawlish felt sorry for her as she stood looking at him, her hands clenched by her sides. She was no fool, although part of the time she had tried to make out that she was. Probably she was afraid of some deep motive, some unknown crime in which the firm, including her father and Mordaunt, was implicated. In spite of that she had hurried ahead of Dawlish, presumably so as to talk to him without letting anyone else know what she intended; had she followed him, the fact would have become known; that suggested that she was seriously afraid that someone at the factory had sent Lank Hair.

If Haling or any of the others learned of their interview at the station, there was a chance that it would be through Lank Hair. If Haling knew, it would be half-way to proving that he had been sent by Haling, and had reported.

'How are you going to explain to Haling and your father what you've done?' Dawlish asked. But before she could answer the telephone rang. Tim went to it.

'It's Dr. Wilson,' Tim reported. 'He wants a word with you.'

Dr. Wilson had promised to keep Dawlish informed of Beresford's progress, but he was calling unexpectedly early. Even then, Dawlish was not particularly alarmed when he went over to the telephone.

'Hallo,' he said, 'what's doing?'

'Beresford is very gravely ill,' said the doctor abruptly, 'and I want to see you at the hospital at once. I hope to save his leg, but he might be lucky if that's all he loses. Will you come?'

CHAPTER ELEVEN

DR. WILSON ASKS QUESTIONS

DAWLISH leapt up the steps of the Bray Street Hospital twenty minutes after Wilson had telephoned him. The bleak hall struck cold. An orderly came hurrying along, calling his name. He stepped forward.

'This way, please, sir, please.'

Dawlish followed quickly, aware of the astringent smell of disinfectants. They climbed two flights of stairs and went along another long passage before the man stopped and tapped at a door.

Wilson answered it. He was writing at a small desk, but stood up at once. He did not smile.

'I'm glad you've been quick, Dawlish.'

'How is he?'

'Neither better nor worse than when I telephoned you. We're trying to save the leg, but it will be touch and go. We may have to amputate, in an attempt to save his life.'

Dawlish said nothing.

Wilson said: 'Look here, Dawlish, you and I know each other fairly well. I've often treated you or your friends for wounds which I should really have mentioned to the police, but I know you're *persona grata* with them and I've always left it to you. I can't, this time.'

'There's no need to,' Dawlish said, 'but why can't you?'

'There's nothing normal about the infection,' Wilson said briefly. 'You say his leg was caught in a trap. Even a rusty and dirty trap wouldn't cause such infection. It doesn't fall into any known category. It's not unlike gangrene, but it's spread too fast and too far for that. What do you know about it?'

'That the wound was caused with malicious intent,' said Dawlish. 'What are you driving at?'

Wilson said slowly: 'I wouldn't say this to anyone but you or the police at this stage, but I'm wondering if the wound was deliberately infected. Something may have been on the jaws of the trap—have you got it?'

'No, I left it where I found it,' said Dawlish. 'May I use the telephone?' He did not wait for an answer, but dialled Scotland Yard. 'Give me Superintendent Trivett, please.' Dawlish held the line for a minute, then went on: 'Bill, this is urgent,' he said, and his tone gave point to his words. 'Will you send two or three men to the patch of waste land at the end of Pymm Place, Wimbledon, to look for a trap.'

'A *what*?' asked Trivett.

'A steel trap,' said Dawlish, 'your men won't mistake it if they see it. I've left it there too long already. I've two men watching the place, so there's just a chance that they may have scared off anyone who's been to get it. Will you do what I ask, and keep the questions for later?'

'All right, where are you speaking from?'

'Bray Street Hospital,' said Dawlish, 'I'm with Dr. Wilson.' He cocked an eye at Wilson, and when that worthy nodded he went on: 'If you yourself can come over here straight away, it would be a help.'

'I'll come,' said Trivett.

Wilson, now satisfied that Dawlish was not working without authority, spoke quietly.

'I might be wrong, of course, and if you can get the trap we should be able to make sure. I don't see how the infection could have been introduced afterwards.'

'I suppose not,' said Dawlish.

He did see a way, although that was not the time to say so. He saw the possibility that Dr. Mordaunt had taken the chance to introduce it. One of the first things to be done was to check up on the reputation of Mordaunt, although he did not seriously think that anything would come from that.

'Is there any point in me seeing Beresford?' he asked.

'No,' said Wilson. 'He wouldn't recognise you, anyhow. I'll keep you posted about his progress.'

'Thanks,' said Dawlish.

He had smoked his third cigarette before Trivett arrived. The policeman and the doctor were old acquaintances, and did not need any introduction.

Wilson nodded, and said much the same as he had to Dawlish. Trivett took it all in very quickly.

'What led up to it?'

Dawlish began to explain what had happened as he and Trivett walked through the long corridors and down the stairs. They went from Bray Street to the flat, with Dawlish talking all the time, so that when they arrived little remained unsaid. They were going up the stairs when he finished:

'And that's as much as I can tell you, Bill. I hope you won't insist on questioning Rene Lampley yet.'

'Why not?'

'If her father and Haling are in this and they think that I'm trying to handle it on my own, they might take chances which they wouldn't with you,' said Dawlish. 'She'll tell them exactly what's happened, there's no doubt of that.'

'I can't leave them very long,' said Trivett. 'I couldn't even if the only information I had was from you.'

'Isn't it?' Dawlish asked, sharply.

'No, I've seen a report from a local policeman at Greenford,' said Trivett. 'As soon as I've a chance I'm going to investigate the odd situation down there. Our man said that he had been talking to the night-watchman at Haling & Haling's factory, and the watchman knew something about the use of the vans. Firewatchers realised the vans were being used, but thought it was an ordinary business. The night-watchman knew better.'

'Presumably because he knew that Haling and the Lampleys were concerned,' said Dawlish. 'I wish it weren't so, Bill.'

'What difference does it make to you?'

Dawlish said: 'If the Lampleys knew that the watchman had told the police, Rene would have known that it would do no harm to elaborate a little. I took her statement as evidence of her innocence, but it no longer stands up.'

'She might not have known about the watchman,' Trivett reminded him.

'The "mights" interest me more than the "might nots",' said Dawlish.

'I suppose so. You certainly get a move on!'

'Bloom has the greater turn of speed just now,' said Dawlish. 'That's a point I can't get over, he sent me to Number 11 Pymm Place, and then arranged for the trap. It can't have been accidental, and it was at the one place where one of us would go. Presumably he expected me to know that the Lampleys were really Penrose's employers. If we put everything together and take the obvious conclusion, the firm is in it right up to the neck. That's right, isn't it?'

'Yes,' said Trivett.

'If we believe Rene Lampley, none of them really know why the vans have been used by night. If we could find that out first, we might have a better starting point.'

'I know of nothing,' said Trivett.

'Yet there must be something, and we now know how very deep Mr. Bloom is,' said Dawlish. 'Well, you're *au fait* with the situation now. If I were handling it, I would take no official action with the Lampleys or the firm. I think it will be much better if they do not think that we are working together, but you may feel that things have changed so much that you'll have to adopt an official attitude.'

'I'll have a word with Morely,' promised Trivett, 'and put your point of view to him.'

'I hope he'll be amenable,' said Dawlish worriedly.

Since he was going to see the Assistant Commissioner before he took any action, Trivett left him at the door of the flat, and he went in alone. Tim was waiting for him in the hall.

'Didn't I hear Trivett?' asked Tim.

'Yes. He's being as helpful as he can.'

'That's just as well,' said Tim quietly. 'Rene's upset at the idea of you contacting the police. Now that she has talked so freely, she's frightened.'

'For herself?'

'I shouldn't think so.'

'We'll have to see Lampley next,' said Dawlish, 'he can't get away with it. I think we'll get Creem and Napier back and then take Rene home ourselves. There hasn't been a telephone call from the Yard, has there?'

'No,' said Tim, and then, after a pause, he asked the question uppermost in his mind. 'How's Ted?'

'So-so,' said Dawlish unhappily.

On second thought, he arranged for Tim to go to Pymm Place and to send Creem and Napier back for a rest; he and Rene were to follow later. He wanted to wait at the flat until he heard whether the trap had been found. He heard Rene and Felicity talking in the drawing-room, and waited in the hall, where there was an extension of the telephone.

The bell rang sharply.

Dawlish answered it, and an operator asked him to hold on while someone inserted the money. So it was not the Yard.

'Ha! ha!' cried a crisp masculine voice. The speaker was Creem, and there was a hint of excitement in his voice. 'I say, Pat, the police are on to something.'

'What?' demanded Dawlish quickly.

'Two plainclothes men came to the plot near the Lampleys' house and took away that trap—and what a trap!'

'So they got it,' said Dawlish with great relief. 'I know, I sent them. I've also sent Tim,' he went on, and explained what he had arranged. Creem said that both he and Napier would be glad of a few hours' sleep, and rang off.

Dawlish telephoned Trivett who had not yet seen Morely. He had received word from his men about the trap. He suggested that Wilson should be allowed to examine the claws and Trivett agreed.

Dawlish was trying to imagine what Bloom really wanted. It was so obvious that he was laying suspicion on the Lampleys and the firm of Haling & Haling that he began to wonder whether it were too obvious.

At last he gave it up and went into the sitting-room.

Felicity and Rene were sitting together, but they had not been talking for some time. Rene looked up quickly when the door opened.

'Have you told the police?' she demanded.

'I haven't done anything that alters the situation,' said Dawlish evasively. 'The next thing I propose to do is to talk to your father, and I want you to come with me. Will you?'

'Yes,' she said at once, 'the sooner it's over the better.'

'I'll come too,' said Felicity.

It was not an arrangement that Dawlish would have planned, but it was better than leaving Felicity alone in the flat. They started on their way, and in three-quarters of an hour they were outside Wimbledon Station. From there they took a bus to Pymm Place.

Tim was waiting near the house.

'Nothing doing,' he said, drawing up to them, 'the place looks empty.'

'It shouldn't be,' said Rene quickly, 'my father was to be in all the afternoon.'

They walked quickly up the short drive. Tim's words had agitated Rene, but Dawlish felt confident that nothing had gone wrong at the house. Creem and Napier had been watching it and they would have reported anything untoward to Tim.

Rene's agitated fingers took some time fumbling for her latch key.

She opened the door at last and stepped inside.

There was no sound, not even a bark from Clam. The absence of a welcome from the terrier seemed to upset Rene, who looked about her uncertainly. Then she called:

'Clam—*Clam!*'

There was no response, no excited yapping. She looked from Dawlish to Tim. Felicity put a hand on her arm.

'Oughtn't the maid to be here?' asked Dawlish.

'No, it's her afternoon off,' said Rene, 'there's only Daddy.' She had gone pale and gave him the impression that something which she had feared had come about. Dawlish moved towards the stairs and said to Tim:

'Look through the kitchen, will you?'

As Tim moved off, Dawlish went up the stairs and Felicity and Rene looked through the downstairs rooms. Dawlish found all the upper rooms empty, but there were no signs of hasty departure. He was retracing his steps when he heard Rene cry out.

It was not a scream; it was an exclamation, startled and horrified, which was broken off short. Other voices followed, and he recognised Felicity's. He hurried down the stairs and met Tim coming from the swing door which led to the domestic quarters.

Neither of the women was in sight.

They hurried to the room from which the voices were coming. The door was ajar and Rene was still talking. She seemed to be muttering to herself, and did not sound normal. Dawlish pushed the door further open, and saw her on her knees beside the terrier.

Felicity glanced round at him, and raised a hand for silence. Clam was dead. Dawlish thought at once that he had been poisoned.

Rene stood up after a long time, her face very pale; but she had herself under control.

'Is anyone in?' she asked.

'We've seen no one,' said Dawlish.

She moved, as if groping her way, to the window and looked out. Dawlish, following the direction of her gaze, could see the clump of trees behind which Beresford had gone to hide.

Her bag lay open, where she had dropped it. A photograph had fallen out and lay face upwards; Dawlish frowned, for it was one of Penrose.

They were still standing there, silently, when the front door-bell rang.

Tim turned towards the door, but Dawlish passed him. He could see the shadow of a man's head and shoulders against the glass, but he had no idea who it might be. He opened the door, and a monstrously fat man stood there, smiling at him.

CHAPTER TWELVE

THE FAT MAN NAMED GEORGE

DAWLISH thought immediately of Bloom.

The fat man's smile faded. It had been set in readiness for the opening of the door, but he was surprised to see Dawlish. Only surprised, he did not appear to be alarmed, and he frowned as he looked past Dawlish along the hall.

'Good afternoon,' said Dawlish.

'Good afternoon,' said the fat man in a pleasant tenor voice. 'I thought—why, Rene, my dear!'

He moved authoritatively towards Rene. She had come from the morning-room, and her expression was brighter; she knew and liked this man. Dawlish watched them shake hands, and heard the fat man say:

'My dear, what is it?'

'Oh *everything's* the matter,' said Rene, with a catch in her voice. 'Clam has been poisoned and Daddy's missing and——'

Words poured out of her. She went back to Dawlish's call on the previous night and her subsequent anxiety, the interview at the office and the attack on the platform. She did not say who Dawlish was nor why he was taking an interest.

The fat man did not interrupt, but he seemed no more aware of the presence of the others than Rene.

When the flow of words at last faltered and stopped, the fat man pursed his lips.

'It is most disturbing, Rene, but I don't think we ought to expect the worst. After all, there might be quite a reasonable explanation of your father's absence, while Clam might have picked up some poison in the garden. Perhaps neither thing is likely, but why should we rule them out in favour of something more melodramatic?'

That was clever; he had discounted his own suggestion and yet made sure that it was planted deeply enough to make the girl clutch at the slender hope.

'I have just come from Charles,' the man went on, 'he told me about the visit of Major Dawlish and he had heard of the incident at the station.'

The fat man turned and looked at Dawlish intently. Had he been thinner, he would have been good-looking; perhaps his most arresting features were his eyes. They were clear, grey, shrewd and frank; the eyes of a man whom Dawlish would normally trust.

Dawlish realised that he must be George, Charles Haling's brother, and decided on a snap question.

'Did Charles ask you about Messrs. Bloom and Blossom?'

He hoped to see some change of expression, but all this man did was to look at him blankly.

'Obviously there is something behind that suggestion, Major Dawlish—you are Dawlish?' Dawlish nodded. 'No, my brother did not mention anyone named Bloom or Blossom. Who are they?'

'Blossom was the man Major Dawlish asked for when he first came here,' said Rene.

'Oh, indeed,' there was a faint smile in the fat man's eyes. 'Apparently you are looking for someone with whom we are not acquainted, Mr. Dawlish. Don't you think it time that you were quite frank?'

'It's past time,' said Dawlish.

'I hardly expected you to say that,' admitted George Haling. 'However, before we go into any matters ourselves, the police must be called. Yes, Rene, I arranged it with Charles, and I came to get your father to agree. As he is not here, the majority of two has it.' He walked into the drawing-room with a swift, light-footed step and lifted the telephone receiver.

'You have no objection to the police being consulted, I trust?' asked George.

'Er—no, none at all,' said Dawlish.

The other could be in no doubt as to his hesitation; the quiet smile proved that. Had he been quite sure of this man's innocence, Dawlish would not have implied that he was not too happy about calling the police, but he was not satisfied. There was a possibility that George Haling and Bloom were one and the same; true, it was a vague one, based only on size, but it was remarkable that two men of such exceptional weight should be implicated in the same case.

If Haling were Bloom, then it was better for him to continue to think that the police were hostile towards Dawlish.

'Is that the police station?' asked Haling. 'Give me Superintendent Weller, please ... this is George Haling.' He held the receiver to his ear and looked deliberately at Dawlish. 'Are you acquainted with the police, Major?'

'Yes.'

'I see. Hallo—Superintendent Weller? It's nice of you to spare me a few minutes, Superintendent. Something rather disturbing but which I hope you will be able to explain quite simply ... Well, the truth is that Arthur Lampley has disappeared ... Yes, I did say disappeared. There might be rather more behind it than that, and I'm afraid that I have been a party to withholding information of importance! ... You won't deal with me too harshly, will you? I had the best of intentions, I assure you! ... in half an hour, excellent. Good-bye.'

He replaced the receiver and smiled at Dawlish.

'Now we should not be long,' he said.

He was a remarkable man, if only because he had stepped into such a situation, with all its attendant emotional stresses and strains, and had contrived to make everything seem quite normal.

'Now, Major Dawlish, we're going to be frank with each other! Shall we start at once, or when the police arrive? You won't mind waiting here until the Superintendent does arrive, will you?' he asked smoothly.

'Not at all,' said Dawlish. He still gave the impression that he felt extremely embarrassed, and that the police were the last people whom he wanted to interview. 'To tell you the truth, Mr. Haling, I have been doing a spot of investigating on my own account.'

'So I gathered from some newspaper reports,' said Haling dryly. 'Vastly amusing, Major Dawlish, when it does not come too close to home. I must admit that I would rather read about your activities than be a victim of them! The truth is that we—I include all the directors of Haling & Haling—have tried to investigate a private mystery ourselves, and because of it we might find our motives misunderstood by the police. I felt that there was a good chance that we would solve our little mystery without help, but now that you have inferred that we are practitioners in crime, it really must become a police matter.'

'Naturally,' said Dawlish, but he still sounded uncertain of himself. 'The police are all right, in their way,' he added, 'but there are cases on which they're slow, you know.'

'What an enormous opinion you have of yourself!' exclaimed George Haling. 'It is really most astonishing!' He smiled at Felicity, as if seeing her for the first time. 'Is this your secretary?'

'My wife,' said Dawlish.

'Oh, indeed,' George bowed slightly. 'And the tall young man who is hovering near the library door in a state of acute embarrassment is one of your bodyguard I suppose? Remarkable!'

It was clear to Dawlish that George Haling was trying to make him lose his temper. The thought occurred to him that, bearing in mind the possibility that George might be Bloom, it might not be a bad idea to fall in with it.

'I don't like your manner!' he snapped, with what he hoped was the right amount of heat. 'I came here to try and help, but if this is your attitude, be damned to you!' He swung on his heel. 'Come, on, Fel—and you, Tim.'

No one spoke. The others went out and Dawlish followed, the picture of injured dignity. With Tim on one side and Felicity on the other he walked down to the gate, but now that he was not visible to Rene or George, he was smiling broadly.

'Did you have to do that?' demanded Tim.

'There was nothing else to do. Haling thinks we're scared of the police, and the local Superintendent will almost certainly agree with him that we're a brace of aggressive and self-opinionated young men who are trying to teach the police their jobs. If Haling is Bloom, that's fine.'

'He doesn't seem the type,' said Tim.

'We don't know what type Bloom is, yet,' Dawlish pointed out, 'and we can't take anything for granted.'

'Supposing Haling isn't Bloom?' asked Felicity.

'Then I think someone in the firm is an associate of Bloom's,' said Dawlish, 'and the information will leak through that way. We haven't done so badly. If it weren't for Ted,' he added with a sudden frown, 'I think I would be enjoying myself!'

'That's fine,' said Tim, 'but have you the faintest idea what to do next?'

'Yes,' said Dawlish. 'This very moment!'

He dived into a wayside telephone kiosk, to Tim's exasperation and Felicity's surprise, and left the door open while he telephoned Elmer Wright. The agency man was in. Dawlish told him in advance that he would be in trouble with the Wimbledon police, and that it was a line which might find some support from one or two of the papers.

'Okay,' said Wright, 'but what about some real dope, Dawlish?'

'I can't give it to you until I've got it,' said Dawlish.

'Can't you tell me what it's about?'

'Not yet, because I don't know,' said Dawlish, 'but patience, old boy, patience.'

'So that's the way it is,' said Wright. 'Okay, I'll see you through.'

'You are a man of great understanding,' said Dawlish.

Tim and Felicity had waited for him, and they looked at him without enthusiasm.

'I don't think you're at your best in this case, darling,' said Felicity. 'All you do is to get yourself in trouble. Have you got any constructive ideas at all?'

'Yes,' said Dawlish. 'I want to get in touch with Bloom. I don't know how to get to him, so he must come to me. It's as simple as that.'

'But he's deliberately lying doggo!' protested Tim.

'Probably,' said Dawlish with a grin, 'but what the devil are you grumbling about? We've unearthed the mystery of the biscuit company's vans, we know that Haling & Haling have something to hide. George's ingenuous frankness might deceive the police, but I think they'll realise that he's got in touch with them because now it would be more dangerous for him not to have done. George may be a junior partner, but he's the power behind this outfit. I wonder how much he weighs?'

'About eighteen stone,' said Tim, judicially, and added: 'but what the blazes does that matter?'

'If we can find out how much Bloom weighs, it would give us a basis for comparison,' said Dawlish with another grin. 'Stop belly-aching, Tim, we can't do any more than we are doing. There isn't any doubt that we're driving them hard. Ted is one example, Lank Hair and the train trick is another. Carr was murdered and Laura was nearly murdered. Two Ats have been killed and there is the curious little monogram—the circle within a star. A man who might or might not have killed the first girl is awaiting trial—in short, there is cause for anxiety and investigation, and we're doing our humble best. We've also forgotten something—or rather, I have.'

'What's that?' asked Felicity quickly.

'There was a night-watchman whose name I don't know, who worked every night for Haling & Co.,' droned Dawlish. 'Whenever he brought them a nice little drink, the watchers promptly fell asleep. Strange that. We could go along to Greenford and try to get his name and address. At least it will satisfy your craving for action, and we needn't bother Trivett,' he added.

'Trivett's probably been out there already,' suggested Felicity gloomily.

She knew, as did the others, that Dawlish was snatching at a straw. There was no angle of the investigation which he could develop on his own. His efforts to bring Bloom into the open had been a failure, although he still hoped that they would bring results. He liked waiting for something to turn up no better than they did, and the thought of visiting the night-watchman was in the way of a forlorn hope.

When they discovered the difficulty of getting to Greenford from Wimbledon by train, they were less anxious to go than ever, and decided to return to the flat for the time being.

It saved them a wasted journey.

Not much more than an hour afterwards, a report was sent into the Greenford police that a man named Browning, a night-watchman at Haling & Haling's Greenford factory, had not been seen that day, and that he had failed to keep several appointments. The house, a small one where he lived alone, was locked up. The police knew of Browning's curious story, and lost no time in investigating.

They found the night-watchman dead.

CHAPTER THIRTEEN

DEAD END

THE decision of George Haling to communicate with the police, together with the murder of the night-watchman, forced Dawlish away from the mystery which he himself had discovered. He had one consolation; now that Haling had sent for the police, his own 'trouble' with them would be more widely known.

There was better news of Ted Beresford, and Wilson now said that he hoped to save his leg as well as his life.

The maw of the steel trap had been examined, but there was no trace of anything which might have caused the infection. Dawlish pondered over the possibility that Dr. Mordaunt was implicated, but Trivett obtained a report on the doctor which could not have been bettered. He had been in the same district for fifteen years, his reputation was as sound as a bell. In answer to Trivett's questions he admitted that he was aware of the mystery of the biscuit company's vans and had been a party to the decision to pursue inquiries privately.

On the afternoon following the day of the discovery of the dead dog and the disappearance of Lampley, Dawlish and Felicity were, in Dawlish's words, at home. Their visitors were Tim, Nathaniel Creem and Charles Napier. A much more composed Laura Desmond had been in for lunch. She had arranged with a relative to stay with her for the time being, and she gave the impression that she was no longer worried.

The flat at Putney was visited by the police again and searched more thoroughly, but nothing came from that. Nothing was found there. Neighbours said that a very fat man had sometimes visited the flat; so had a man who answered the description of the lank-haired man, but nothing was learned about them. The owner of the taxi service which Bloom had used in Kingston was interrogated. Bloom had ordered the taxi by telephone and had kept it all day. The driver described him as a 'very fat bloke'.

'And there we have a chance or two of making sure whether Bloom or George Haling are one and the same,' said Dawlish. 'We can't do it ourselves, because Bill's looking after it.'

'Do you think he'll get results?' asked Tim lazily.

'I doubt it,' admitted Dawlish. 'We seem to be at a completely dead end.'

Not long afterwards Trivett rang through to say that the taxi-driver had seen George Haling, and was quite sure that his fare on the day of the murder had been a different man; they were much of a size, but had no other similarities.

'So that appears to be that,' said Dawlish glumly.

'I'm afraid so,' admitted Trivett. 'Things aren't going well for you, Pat.'

'You sound remarkably sympathetic,' said Dawlish.

'I feel it,' said Trivett. 'You've uncovered a lot that we didn't know before.'

'For that crumb of comfort, many thanks,' said Dawlish. 'You did know, indirectly—if you'd followed up Penrose's employers you would have got to Haling & Haling.'

'That's a sore point,' admitted Trivett. 'We did follow up, but we didn't discover that there was anything unusual about them. Now, of course, we know that the Halings might have looked after Penrose's defence because they know for certain that he is innocent, but we're going to have a difficult job to prove that.'

'Yes. What about Lampley?'

'There's still no trace of him.'

'Got any idea of how the dog was poisoned?'

'Yes. He'd eaten meat with morphine in it,' said Trivett. 'We've been through that house with a fine-toothed comb, believe me, but found nothing.'

'Are the Halings and Rene being helpful?'

'Now that they've told us about it, they couldn't make themselves more so,' said Trivett.

'Hum,' said Dawlish darkly. 'Any clue as to why the vans were used or where they went?'

'None,' said Trivett. 'It's pretty difficult to get vans identified when they've only been on the road after dark, you know.'

'You needn't rub in the difficulties,' said Dawlish with a rueful grin. 'As we have said, it's a dead end. About the nightwatchman, by the way—why do you think he was killed?'

'So that he couldn't give evidence that he had doped the drinks which the Halings and the Lampleys had when they sat up to watch,' said Trivett.

'At least we agree about that,' said Dawlish.

He rang off and passed on Trivett's news. It permitted only one explanation. Every effort was being made to make it look as if the firm of Haling & Haling were implicated; everything which they might bring up as evidence in their favour was being destroyed or removed.

'Trivett thinks so, too, although he did not put it into words,' said Dawlish. 'Is there another cup of tea, Fel?'

Felicity peered into the tea-pot absently. 'Pat, aren't they trying to make the Haling firm too obvious?'

'That's a point worth thinking about,' said Dawlish. 'It's just possible that one or more of the directors of the firm are implicated and are trying to foist the blame on to the others. Except for that letter of Smythe's, though, there's no direct connection between Haling & Haling and the murders. Do you know what I think?' he added thoughtfully.

'I see that you are about to tell us, whether we do or not,' said Jeremy lazily.

'How right you are. Here goes, then. I think that Smythe was sent along with the copy of the letter in his pocket to make sure that we looked into Haling & Haling. Whether George has undermined the plans by bringing in the police is a different matter. Bloom may have hoped that we would go for Haling & Haling, without confiding in the police.' He grinned. 'He might even have kidded himself that it was safe for us to investigate the affairs of the company, but that the police, as experts, would come across something of interest. However—all this is just talk.'

81

'Just talk,' admitted Tim.

Dawlish sipped his tea with slow enjoyment.

'Look here,' said Tim, after a long silence, 'we can't just sit back and admit that we've been bamboozled!'

'Certainly not,' said Dawlish, 'we must all think deep thoughts. Somewhere along the line we've travelled there is something to give us an opening, but we've missed.'

'Penrose?' suggested Felicity.

Dawlish went on smoking for a moment or two, and then put his pipe down with a certain deliberation.

'You may have got something there, Fel. Penrose it is. I think I'll get Trivett to give me permission to see him.'

'Why?' asked Tim.

Dawlish said: 'It's a long shot, but let's put it this way: the crooks have worked for a long time through Haling & Haling. Penrose knows something, wittingly or unwittingly, which might lead to their undoing. Therefore, they frame Penrose.'

Having partially convinced himself, Dawlish leapt up from his chair, calling out loud good-byes as he reached the door.

He decided to walk to Scotland Yard, hoping that someone was sufficiently interested to follow him, but there was no indication of this; Bloom seemed to have written him off. It would not be long before Elmer Wright asked for something more definite than he had so far received. Gloom settled over Dawlish, who concentrated on the thought that with the proper trend of questioning Penrose might remember something which would start the hunt again. The man was lodged at Brixton Prison and Dawlish did not think that he would have much difficulty in getting Trivett's permission to visit him.

Alan Penrose was alone in his cell.

The newspaper photograph which Dawlish had seen did not do him justice. Even after several weeks of waiting, he looked fit and well. There was no hint of depression about him as he sat reading. One of the things which Trivett had remarked upon was that the accused man did not seem to be in the slightest degree worried about the result of the trial. He had steadfastly maintained his innocence, had given the police every possible help, and yet he could not deny the circumstances which had made his arrest imperative.

He was considered a model prisoner, and he was given certain privileges. Men such as Penrose who were awaiting trial for murder had sympathetic treatment from the warders and prison officials in any case, and Penrose was better treated than most.

It was nearly six o'clock on a warm evening, and at six the cell doors would be opened and he would be allowed a walk in the yard. Presently he heard the footsteps of his jailers, closed the book and stood up.

'Good evening, sir.'

'Hallo,' said Penrose, unaware that 'sir' was a courtesy reserved for very special prisoners. Certainly he had an air about him, and the smile on his pleasant face was friendly. 'Have you come to give me another airing?'

'Yes, sir.'

'Good!' Penrose, dressed in battle-dress, followed the warder along the passages to a prison yard. There was a single door in the wall, which was eight feet high and surmounted by spikes and barbed wire, and from a corner window in the prison building an armed warder was on constant watch. Every part of the wall was visible from the window, but the door leading from the prison was not.

The warder offered cigarettes.

'Thanks,' said Penrose. 'You know, prison life isn't as bad as it's painted!'

'That's good, sir,' said the warder, a stolid man who felt extremely sorry for this prisoner; he had followed the evidence in the Press and did not think that Penrose had a chance in a million of getting off. Yet he did not believe this man capable of cold-blooded murder. He was of the opinion that he could not take his liquor well, and that the girl who had been killed had been a provocative little piece who had invited trouble.

Unaware of the warder's ruminations, Penrose strolled about the courtyard, enjoying the brief relaxation. Suddenly he heard other footsteps and looked round to see a second warder and an officer in uniform. The officer wore a clerical collar.

The second warder retired, the first moved away to a discreet distance.

'Well, Penrose, how are you today?' asked the padre heartily. He shook hands. 'It's nice to see you taking the air!'

'They look after me very well here, sir,' said Penrose.

'I'm glad to hear it. Oh, warder!—just a moment.'

The warder approached them smartly, and then stopped

aghast, for the man in padre's uniform was covering him with a small automatic.

'If you shout, I shall kill you,' he said.

The heartiness had gone from his voice, which was now clipped and threatening. The warder gulped, and Penrose said:

'What on earth——'

'Be quiet, Penrose! I shan't harm him if he's obedient. Take off your uniform,' he snapped to the man.

'But——' began Penrose.

The warder opened his mouth, but before he uttered a cry the 'padre' brought the butt of his automatic sharply down on his head. The man collapsed without a sound. The 'padre' swung round and snapped:

'Come on, don't be a fool!'

In less than five minutes Penrose was dressed in the warder's clothes. No one else entered the courtyard. When ready, Penrose once drew back, as if still uncertain, but the other covered him with the gun, and said:

'This is the only way, Penrose.'

Then he led the way into the prison.

He obviously knew it well, for he chose a passage which was rarely used and reached a side entrance in a few seconds. On the way he snapped instructions; he would do the talking, Penrose had only to keep silent and to follow him.

Penrose obeyed.

It was incredibly easy at first. Two warders saluted the padre, who boomed a greeting, and kept up a running conversation with Penrose. Approaching the main gates, he looked rapidly to right and left.

Then, without warning, a burst of shooting started from the road.

CHAPTER FOURTEEN

THE ESCAPE

THERE was a closed car with a man at the wheel and another in the back, outside the gates of the prison. The rear door was open. The man dressed as a padre rushed towards the car, dragging Penrose with him. From right and left other men came running, all carrying guns; there were two small cars along the road.

There was no doubt of the gunmen's purpose.

They were there to create a disturbance and so facilitate Penrose's escape, and they succeeded. Few people were passing, and those who were in sight were too scared to do anything.

It was then that a taxi drew up. The passenger was Dawlish carrying a permit to see Penrose.

He saw a man in the uniform of a warder being pushed into a car and an army padre climbing in after him; the padre held a gun. Dawlish caught one glimpse of the 'warder's' face, and recognised Penrose.

'Strewth!' gasped the taxi-driver, 'there's a ruddy riot!'

'Ten pounds if you'll follow that large car,' Dawlish shouted to him through the pandemonium.

The car was already moving away from the kerb but there was still shooting, directed towards the gates of the prison and intended to make pursuit impossible.

The taxi-driver started his engine.

'Twenty!' he shouted back.

'Twenty!' agreed Dawlish.

The man did not speak again, but slipped in his clutch and the taxi roared off. It passed the two small cars and the scene by the gates; no one seemed to suspect that a taxi might be playing a part in this wild affray. The private car, a Hillman, swung round the corner towards the left and then hared off towards Streatham.

Dawlish sat back, but he took out his automatic.

He was in civilian clothes, but he had carried a gun from the time Carr had been shot. Now he watched the Hillman as it gathered speed. The taxi was travelling at nearly sixty miles an hour, but the Hillman was pulling away.

The driver of the taxi kept on grimly.

Dawlish did not know whether the passengers in the Hillman realised that they were being followed, but if they did not they would soon discover it. He had little doubt that they would shoot as soon as they thought there was any serious danger.

On the wide roads across the Common the Hillman increased its speed. The taxi managed to keep pace, although the driver's face was getting anxious. Soon they were heading for Wandsworth along East Hill and then towards Putney.

Obviously the police had been warned of the madly-driven car, for there were numerous attempts to stop them. Once a police car swerved across the path of the Hillman in an attempt to force it into the kerb, but the Hillman, superbly driven, squeezed through to safety.

The taxi followed.

'Good work!' exclaimed Dawlish, leaning forward tensely.

'You'll 'ave to pension me orf,' shouted the driver, 'I won't never keep my licence arter this!'

They roared up Putney Hill and swung left at the top, but the Hillman was foxing. Instead of going towards Wimbledon it turned right and then went sharp left and took the Roehampton Road.

Roehampton's narrow streets nearly brought disaster, but they managed to squeeze through oncoming traffic and were soon heading for the Kingston by-pass. Obviously the Hillman driver now knew that he was being followed; he was taking the narrow roads and the longer way round in the hope of shaking the taxi off.

They were half-way along the by-pass when a man leaned out of the window of the Hillman and fired. The faint yellow sparks of colour were clearly visible, but the bullets went wide. If the taxi-driver knew what they were doing, he ignored it.

The hand holding the gun suddenly disappeared; there seemed to be confusion in the car although Dawlish could not see what was happening. It began to swerve along the road, straightened out, then swerved again.

The taxi gained on it.

The driver turned round as Dawlish leaned forward.

'They're goin' to crash if they're not careful,' he said. 'What do we do now?'

'Keep your eyes peeled,' said Dawlish.

The Hillman began to swerve in wild gyrations, suddenly Dawlish realised what was happening; the men inside the car were struggling! He could see heads and arms moving, and thought he could discern a man leaning over the back of the driver.

Then the Hillman crashed.

The driver had seemed to have regained control and it had started to increase its speed; then it swerved, failed to straighten, and struck a telegraph pole broadside on. It swung right round the pole and ended up facing the taxi.

The taxi slowed down as if this were a normal enough business.

'This right, sir?' the driver demanded.

'First-rate!' said Dawlish with enthusiasm.

He saw a door of the Hillman open and was prepared for more shooting. Instead, the man in the dress of the prison warder got out. He looked shaken, but appeared to be unhurt. He stood staring in some bewilderment as Dawlish jumped from the taxi and approached him. There was a little group of people further along the road, but none immediately opposite them.

Inside the car the driver was slumped over the wheel and the padre's body lay motionless in the back.

Dawlish said: 'There isn't time for talking now, but I'm a friend of some friends of yours.'

'Oh,' said Penrose.

The spectators were getting nearer, and there was a policeman among then. Penrose looked tight-lipped at Dawlish, but did not speak. Here was an impasse and Dawlish had an exasperating feeling that there was something to do and that he had missed it. The truth was that he was confused by the fact that Penrose had struggled with the men who had liberated him, and was now waiting here and making no effort to get away. Before the spectators and the police could get any closer, he took Penrose's arm and rushed him towards the taxi, saying:

'Get in—I'll see you through!'

He thought Penrose was going to object, but the man climbed in and Dawlish snapped to the driver:

'Scotland Yard, in a hurry!'

That worked.

The people nearby held back, even the policeman looked startled, while the driver had not the slightest hesitation in starting off again. Before anyone realised what was happening, he had turned in the road and the taxi was rattling back at a fine pace.

Penrose was breathing hard.

Dawlish said: 'You are Penrose, aren't you?'

'Yes.'

'Look at that,' said Dawlish, 'and then do what I say, will you?'

He showed Penrose his official Intelligence card.

It seemed obvious that *Penrose did not want to be rescued*; the scrum in the car made that clear. It had also dawned upon him that probably Bloom wanted the man, and, therefore, that he was an important witness. Just how those circumstances could be turned to best advantage he did not know, but he did not doubt that it could be done.

Penrose looked at him, frowning.

'You're Major Dawlish?'

'Yes, but there's no time for explanations,' said Dawlish. 'We're not going to the Yard, I'll see the police after we've tucked you away safely.' He judged from Penrose's expression that he was likely to argue, and went on quickly: 'This is the only way we'll find out what's happening. The murder they're trying to blame on you is one of a series.'

'A—*series*!' exclaimed Penrose.

'That's right,' said Dawlish, putting a hand on the other's knee. 'Don't be awkward, and don't ask questions just now.'

Penrose looked completely bewildered.

Dawlish sat back, wondering how the driver would take a change of instructions and also how he could get Penrose somewhere safe and not too far away. He ran through a list of acquaintances who lived on this side of London. By then they were approaching the end of the by-pass.

He could think of no one.

It would not be long before the taxi was stopped; its number would have been noted and directly they were in a built-up area again the police would recognise it. There was still a chance of getting to Wimbledon Common and out towards Epsom, or even Croydon.

Croydon.

He leaned forward and put his card through the window, sticking it in front of the driver's nose. The man read it, and turned to give Dawlish a wide grin.

'Okay, sir.'

'I hope it is,' said Dawlish. 'Have you enough petrol to get to Croydon?'

'I thought you said——'

'I did, but I've changed my mind,' said Dawlish. 'Can you get to Croydon?'

'Just about,' said the driver dubiously. 'I dunno whether I

ought to, sir, I—o-kay!' he broke off, when Dawlish waved the card in front of him again, 'but if you let me dahn, guv'nor, I'll be broke fer life.'

'I won't let you down,' promised Dawlish.

Near Croydon lived Dr. William Farningham, who had often worked with Dawlish and Ted Beresford. Farningham had been in the army, had been wounded in Italy and had since returned to civilian life. He had a practice at Sanderstead, where he lived with his wife. He would jump at the chance of helping. Once at his house Dawlish would have time to work out the details of the subterfuge which had sprung to mind when he had carried Penrose off.

Dawlish sat back in the taxi and offered cigarettes. Penrose seemed glad to smoke. He drew hard at the cigarette and looked sideways at Dawlish.

'I suppose you do know what you're doing?' he said.

'Oh, I think so.'

'Because I'm only making it worse for myself by staying away from the police,' said Penrose. 'I'd no idea what was coming. I——'

'Nine times out of ten you would be right, but this is the tenth,' said Dawlish. 'In any case you're not staying away from the police, because I am working with them.' He did not know whether Penrose would accept that statement on its face value, but it aroused no comment. 'I can't go into details now,' said Dawlish, 'and you'll have to take my word for it. I'll give you one assurance; within two hours of reaching Croydon, Superintendent Trivett will either come to see you or telephone you.'

'Oh,' said Penrose. 'I know Trivett.'

'Good. Are you feeling happier about it?'

'I feel helplessly confused,' admitted Penrose, drawing in his breath. 'It's been the craziest hour of my life! Can't you explain anything?'

Dawlish paused to marshal his thoughts. Then: 'I can tell you that in common with a lot of other people, I don't think that you murdered Clara Stuart. On the other hand the case against you is so strong that without new evidence you will probably be convicted.'

'That's what I can't believe,' said Penrose. 'Confound it, I *didn't* kill her!'

'The evidence is there,' said Dawlish, 'but since you were arrested, the case has got rather more complicated. There have been several other murders, although none directly connected with the one with which you're charged. I'll go into further details later, but just now you'll have to be satisfied with the fact that you are what we might call a pawn in a very big game.'

'I see,' said Penrose.

He did not seem altogether satisfied, but he did not insist on a further explanation. The curious thing about Penrose was that he did not appear to be greatly affected by the ordeal of awaiting trial.

The fact that he could sit back without talking was an indication of that.

They were soon through Croydon and approaching Sanderstead. Dawlish gave the driver instructions on how to reach Farningham's house, and hoped that his friend would be in. When the cab drew up outside it was nearly eight o'clock. From the back of the house came the rattle of a lawn-mower.

'This is where you put up for the night,' said Dawlish, and climbed out.

CHAPTER FIFTEEN

FARNINGHAM IS HELPFUL

DAWLISH gave the taxi-driver his card, on which he scribbled a note to Trivett, and advised him to go straight to Scotland Yard with it. He also gave the man five five-pound notes, and sent him off jubilantly.

Penrose looked curiously at Dawlish.

'I seem to remember your face.'

'Some people do,' said Dawlish absently. 'Let's go round to the back, I've a feeling that there is much hard work being done in the garden.'

Bill Farningham, a man of rather more than medium height, could undoubtedly be classed among the not-so-thin. This was a fact he deplored, and could have been the reason why he was so arduously pushing a small mower over a large lawn.

He paused to wipe his forehead as Dawlish came in sight.

'Pat, confound you, why didn't you give me a ring?'

'Pressing circumstances prevented me,' said Dawlish, as they shook hands. 'I thought doctors were so busy that they couldn't get five minutes away from their patients!'

'I have an hour in the garden every evening,' said Farningham with a grin, 'and none of my patients are tactless enough to need attention between half-past seven and half-past eight!' He smiled at Penrose.

'Alan Penrose,' said Dawlish, glancing at Penrose, 'the latest man to escape from Brixton.'

'I——' began Penrose.

'Congratulations! All by yourself?'

'No,' said Penrose dazedly, 'I——'

'It's no easy job, even with help,' said Farningham, as if seriously. 'So you're up to your tricks again, Pat? I thought I read something between the lines of the gossip pars. In fact I was going to give you a ring some time.'

'A flattering delusion,' said Dawlish. 'Do you mind if we take the escaped prisoner out of the garden? Your neighbours might get curious about his uniform.'

'Of course. Come in.' Farningham led the way to the house. 'I'm sorry that Joyce isn't here—she's away for a few days. You would choose a time when she can't tell you what an oaf you are, wouldn't you?'

'Are you on your own?' asked Dawlish.

'Oh, no, we've been lucky,' said Farningham, 'we've a treasure plus a daily, so we live in state.'

'I expect she'll be able to rustle something up.'

He had a short consultation with the treasure in the kitchen, and then herded the other two on into the living-room.

All comfortably settled with drinks Farningham turned to Penrose. 'Well,' he said, affably, 'how long have you known Dawlish?'

'Quite long enough,' said Penrose with feeling. 'About fifty minutes to an hour, and he's got me absolutely flummoxed!'

'Oh, that's his usual way of behaving,' said Farningham. 'Have you really come from Brixton?'

'You'll be able to hear about it on the nine o'clock news,' said Dawlish. 'Bill, I want to leave Penrose here for the night, at least. Trivett will be coming out to see him, so it's all above board. As a matter of fact, queer things have been happening——'

He went into some details about the attempted rescue, his theories and what had preceded the prison incident.

Farningham took it all in so matter-of-fact a fashion that Penrose stared at him, as if fascinated. Dawlish contrived to make his decision to outwit Bloom seem eminently reasonable.

When he finished, Penrose said:

'But why should this man Bloom want to rescue me?'

'That's what we have to find out,' said Dawlish. 'By tomorrow morning, at the latest, he will know that you're with me, and if that doesn't fetch him, nothing will. Now it's your turn,' he added.

Penrose began to speak quietly and with no sense of panic.

He told his story well.

He had not known the 'padre' when with his unit; the man had told him that he was newly-posted, and had been requested to look after Penrose. The man had made several visits to the prison, but said nothing to suggest what was going to happen that day. Penrose admitted that when the man had first offered him the chance to escape he had been too surprised to resist, but once near the gates, when the shooting had started, he had been given no choice.

'After the padre started shooting at you out of the window, I managed to knock the fellow out, there was a bit of a struggle, and—well, you know what happened.'

'I do, indeed. Now I'd better give Trivett a ring.'

Dawlish left a message for Trivett at the Yard and settled down to wait. During a substantial and extremely well-cooked meal he told Penrose and Farningham more of the story. Farningham seemed to derive pleasure from it, but Penrose grew more and more sober. That was not surprising, and Dawlish watched for the man's reaction.

The curious impression that Penrose was inwardly quite composed and confident remained, and he liked the man. He thought that Bloom wanted something from him or he would not have gone to such extravagant lengths to get him out of Brixton; but Penrose gave no indication of what it might be.

Finally, Dawlish approached the matter directly.

'Well, you know pretty well all that I can tell you, Penrose. Now it's your turn.'

'*I* can do nothing,' Penrose assured him.

'Bloom thinks that you can.'

'If I know anything of interest to a man of that calibre, I'm quite unaware of it,' said Penrose earnestly.

Dawlish was about to talk for the first time of the circle within a star, when the front doorbell rang. Presently Trivett's voice was heard in the hall. As he entered the room Dawlish watched Penrose closely.

The man looked frankly enough into Trivett's eyes, but did not speak. Trivett nodded to Dawlish, and Farningham, and stared at Penrose. There was a long silence, until Trivett spoke quietly.

'How did you get here, Penrose?'

'Major Dawlish brought me.'

'I know that. How did you make arrangements with the other people so as to break away?'

'I did not.'

Trivett looked sceptical, but Dawlish insisted on taking up the story. He missed out nothing of what Penrose had told him.

Trivett listened without interrupting, and then said:

'Do you seriously believe all this, Dawlish?' The use of the surname proved that he was not going to allow Dawlish to take advantage of their friendship; it was his way of saying that the matter was now formal.

Dawlish frowned.

'Most certainly I do,' he said.

'What makes you so sure?'

'Because Penrose came with me willingly. Because he was instrumental in crashing the car and thereby risked personal injury, and because it's about the most unlikely story I've ever heard,' added Dawlish with a grin. 'Did you get the two other men in the car?'

'Yes.'

'Have they talked?'

'One won't, the other can't—he's unconscious and in hospital.' Trivett's manner was slightly thawing. 'It's asking a lot to expect me to believe such an incredible rigmarole,' he said, 'and yet——'

'It is perfectly true,' said Penrose, 'and it is equally true that I did not kill Clara Stuart.'

Trivett looked at him evenly, and then said:

'Dawlish, spare me a few minutes privately, will you?'

'Of course,' said Dawlish. 'Can we use the dining-room?' He looked at Farningham, who agreed at once, and then led the way out. Trivett looked a little uneasy as he closed the door and wondered aloud whether there was any likelihood of Penrose attacking Farningham and trying to get away.

'Not a chance at all,' Dawlish assured him.

'What makes you feel so sure?'

'The same thing which has made you doubtful about the man's guilt,' said Dawlish. 'He's genuine and he's sincere.'

'He might have been under the influence of drink when the girl was murdered,' Trivett pointed out.

'He wasn't under the influence of drink this evening,' said Dawlish decisively.

'But for him, the Hillman would have got away and you wouldn't now have the other two men in custody.'

Trivett said: 'The warder's evidence supports his story, but even if I believe you, I can't hope to convince others.'

'We'll have to find a way, and the warder's evidence will help,' said Dawlish. 'I've set all the traps for Bloom that I can think of, but I've never had a piece of bait as persuasive as this. You must let me hold on to him for a day or two, Bill.'

'It's utterly impossible!' said Trivett. 'Confound it, the man is on trial for murder!'

'He's on trial for a murder which strikes far deeper than was at first realised,' said Dawlish. 'If Morely can't see that Penrose is our only hope, then he's getting senile. I might have dodged off with the prisoner and let you whistle to find him, but I thought you'd better know about it. However, it isn't too late. I'll get him somewhere else without telling you where he is, if your professional conscience is worrying you.'

'No,' said Trivett decisively. 'You can't get away with it, Pat. You had your chance. Surely you know that once you brought me here I'd have to take him away with me? There are limits to how far I can stretch regulations; even you should know that.'

'Against red tape even the gods fight in vain!' misquoted Dawlish bitterly.

'Well then, how do you expect me to?' said Trivett with grim humour.

'All right, Bill,' said Dawlish abruptly, 'but it's on your own head. Penrose will act like a magnet on Bloom unless I'm greatly mistaken. Once you get him back——' He stopped, and a new light shone in his eyes. 'But Bill, no one need *know* that he's in custody again, need they?'

'Well——' began Trivett.

'It's getting dark,' went on Dawlish excitedly, 'and in an hour no one will be able to see who goes in or out. Bloom won't know that I brought Penrose here, so you can have your prisoner and still let me have the chance of a chat with Bloom.'

Trivett looked at him oddly.

'*Now* what's on your mind?' demanded Dawlish.

'I suppose you're sure that this man Bloom exists,' said Trivett slowly.

Dawlish regarded Trivett without expression. The silence lengthened. Trivett broke it with a slight, embarrassed cough.

'Well, well!' exclaimed Dawlish. 'Who's put that idea into your head? A man who calls himself Bloom exists all right. He might be George Haling under another guise——'

'Our witness——'

'Hush!' exhorted Dawlish. 'Even fat men can dye their hair and fill out their cheeks and generally adopt disguise which would deceive anyone who doesn't know them well. Your witness saying that Bloom—or our fat man at Putney—and Haling are not the same wouldn't stand up for three minutes under a keen cross-examination, and you know it. You also know that Carr was shot and that the fat man did exist——'

Trivett broke in: 'We've your word for it and your information came from Mrs. Desmond, didn't it? You didn't actually see him yourself?'

'Now, come! A fat man hired a taxi all day. Confound it, you've gone to the trouble to check up!'

'A fat man hired the taxi, a fat man was near Penrod's, a fat man was a visitor to Smythe,' admitted Trivett, 'but there is no evidence that it is one and the same man and still less that he is concerned in this affair. I'm sorry, Pat, but I have to look at it that way. I'm not the only one who has wondered, as you can imagine.'

'Oh,' said Dawlish. 'I see Cousin Archie's busy little mind has been putting two and two together and making five again. Well, I suppose I can't blame either of you, but you can stake your last penny that there *is* a man who has called himself Bloom, and that we'll find him before this show is over. What do you want from me? My resignation?'

'Now, come——' began Trivett.

'Now, come! Be reasonable, Pat old boy!' There was more than a touch of bitterness in Dawlish's voice. 'Confound it, old chap, we're sorry about it, and all that but we can't let you go on the rampage any longer!

'All in all, I think perhaps you're right. This is no country for the persecution of unorthodox crooks. Let them do all the routine crimes in the routine way, and you can cope, but here you have an innocent man practically condemned as a murderer, a series of crimes which you're more or less prepared to brush under the carpet, and you're flummoxed. I'm flummoxed, too, but at least I've the wit to see that something nasty is brewing.'

'I'm sorry, Pat.'

'You've every cause to be,' said Dawlish. 'All right, go off with Penrose, and if you've any sense, keep his recapture dark. The papers know about the escape, I expect. Let them run the story. If there's a stop press tomorrow morning saying that he's been recaptured it will be the worst day's work you've ever done.'

'I think I'll telephone the A.C.' said Trivett doubtfully.

'Well, that's a concession,' said Dawlish.

There was a telephone in the hall, and Trivett dialled the Yard, while Dawlish went in to join Penrose and Farningham. They could tell by his expression that things had not gone well.

'You'll be going back, Penrose. I hoped to keep you here for a little while, but——' he broke off and shrugged his shoulders.

'I thought you were connected with the police,' said Penrose.

'I was,' said Dawlish, bitterly, 'but it will be a long time before I raise a finger to help them again.' He shrugged his shoulders. 'That will probably be a great relief and benefit to all concerned!' He lit a cigarette, listened to the murmur of Trivett's voice on the telephone, and then took a pencil from his pocket and began to draw on the edge of a newspaper. Before he had finished Trivett came in.

'We'll hold over the announcement of the recapture until tomorrow morning,' he said, 'which means that it won't get in the Press until early afternoon. That's about what you want, isn't it?'

'It's better than I'd hoped from the depths of my depression,'
admitted Dawlish, relief lighting up his general gloom. 'Treat
Penrose kindly, won't you? It wasn't his fault that they came
for him, you know. I suppose you *do* believe that a gang of
gunmen held up the guards at Brixton Prison this evening?
That it wasn't all imagination?'

'Don't be an ass,' said Trivett.

'Well——'

'It's the question of Bloom's identity which is worrying us,'
said Trivett, more expansive than Dawlish expected him to be in
front of Penrose.

He broke off, and Dawlish smiled faintly.

'All right, all right. You'll leave after dark?'

'Yes. Munk will be along.'

'I'd forgotten the amiable sergeant,' said Dawlish. He
finished a drawing which Trivett's return had interrupted and
regarded it for some seconds in silence. Then he pushed the
paper into Penrose's hand.

'Have you ever seen that sign before?'

There followed a curious moment.

Penrose's expression suddenly hardened. He did not speak for
a moment, and when he did, his voice was pitched on a low
key.

'What does this mean?'

'That is our problem,' said Dawlish. 'It's the secret cypher of
Mr. Bloom, as far as we can make out. Why? Do you recognise
it?'

'Of course I recognise it,' said Penrose.

CHAPTER SIXTEEN

THE TRADE MARK

'WELL, what is it?' asked Dawlish.

The question broke a few seconds of complete silence. Penrose had been staring at the sign, and the others at Penrose. He
was obviously affected, and he did not answer immediately.

'It's a trade mark,' Penrose said at last.

'Whose?' asked Dawlish.

'It hasn't been registered,' said Penrose, 'but it was to have been the trade mark of a certain brand of biscuit my firm was to have put on the market just before the outbreak of war. As I designed it, I didn't know that anyone else had seen it. How did you get hold of it?'

Dawlish said: 'Penrose, you aren't telling the whole truth, you know. There isn't a hope of saving your life unless you do so. It's now apparent that you have been cleverly framed for the murder of Clara Stuart, and the use of this mark, which you have originated, is calculated to worsen your position. Only the whole truth will help you, by enabling the police and me to find out what is really behind it.'

Penrose said: 'I am telling the truth.'

He would not say anything more, although Dawlish was convinced that he was keeping something back, and Trivett looked as if he was of the same opinion. Dawlish tried another tack, and learned that the board of directors of Haling & Haling, as well as the manager and the secretary, knew of the mark.

By then it was quite dark.

A chiming clock struck ten.

'I think we'll get off,' said Trivett. 'I'll be back in a moment.' He went out.

Dawlish saw at once that Trivett was giving him an opportunity of questioning Penrose while he was away. He said quickly:

'Penrose, we've a couple of minutes at the most. I am not a policeman, and I'm trying to help you. What do you really know about that trade mark?'

Penrose looked at him levelly.

'First you say you are working with the police. Then you say you are not. It's quite obvious that you have some other interest. What *do* you want?' His voice was harsh and bitter.

Dawlish said: 'I want to find out who murdered Clara Stuart and at least three other people. I also want to know why the vans belonging to Haling & Haling were used after dark.'

Penrose drew in his breath.

'So you knew about that,' said Dawlish. 'Time's flying, remember. I won't tell the police what you tell me, providing it does not implicate you in the murders. Don't play the fool any longer.' He was on edge in case Trivett came back, and his ears were strained to catch the sound of footsteps.

Penrose said: 'I didn't kill Clara. I knew that she had this tattoo mark, and so did a friend of hers. I saw it when we went to the swimming baths together a few weeks ago. It worried me, because I couldn't imagine how they came by it. I tried to persuade Clara to tell me why she had it, but she wouldn't. It was about the trade mark that we quarrelled on the night that she was killed.'

'Oh,' said Dawlish. 'And were you overheard?'

'Could have been, I suppose.'

'Why are you so anxious not to tell the police about that?'

There was the sound of a footstep in the hall.

Dawlish motioned to Farningham, who slipped out of the door, closing it quickly. They could hear him talking to Trivett, and gaining precious time.

'Out with it!' Dawlish urged.

Penrose drew in his breath.

'Haling & Haling are a wonderful firm,' he said. 'They've treated me and my family with the utmost consideration. Only people to whom I owe a great deal could know about the trade mark. There is some mystery which affects them. I've heard about the mystery of the vans, too, it's obviously to do with the bigger trouble, but if *my* safety is dependent upon getting either of the Halings, Lampley or the other people there into trouble, I don't want to be safe.'

He spoke without any suggestion of histrionics or noble self-sacrifice, but he made it clear that he thought one of the people for whom he had so great a devotion was deeply involved. It was no time for arguing about his wisdom.

Dawlish made up his mind quickly.

'All right,' he said, 'I'll do what I can and the police needn't know about this yet. Now listen to me. There's just a chance that you can escape from Trivett and the other police when you get outside. Will you take it?'

'Why?' demanded Penrose.

'I think it will help,' said Dawlish. He thrust his hand into his trouser pocket and drew out a handful of silver, pushed it into Penrose's hand then added some notes from his wallet. 'Get to Arum Cottage, Basingstoke—it's a mile or so out on the

99

Newbury road. Give my name and tell the people there that I sent you, but don't mention the place if you're caught.'

Farningham could be heard talking loudly, obviously trying to cover what was being said in the room. The door began to open. Penrose did not speak, but thrust the money into his pocket, as Trivett came in.

'Come along, Penrose. I should warn you that my men outside are armed, and have instructions to shoot if you try to get away.'

Penrose nodded, and moved to the door.

Dawlish did not go out with them. Farningham hesitated, looking back at Dawlish, who stared hard-faced ahead of him. The footsteps of the two men sounded loud in the hall, then more sharply on the stone porch. Vague sounds followed, gradually fading.

'What——' began Farningham.

Suddenly there came to them the tattoo of running footsteps, and then the sharp report of a pistol shot. Farningham hurried to the door, but Dawlish stayed where he was, a quiet smile on his lips.

Two or three more shots were followed by an excited chorus of comment. That died away, and the room became very quiet.

Trivett strode back into the house.

'Did you have to do that?' he demanded harshly.

'Do what?' asked Dawlish curiously.

'Prompt Penrose to escape.'

'I did little more than hope that he would,' said Dawlish mendaciously. 'Did he get away?' He tried to show no great interest, but his heart was hammering against his ribs. He was afraid that Penrose might be either badly wounded or killed, but there was no way of telling from Trivett's expression.

'Yes,' Trivett said, 'and you'll have to answer for it.' He turned on his heel without another word.

There were a few minutes of quiet before Farningham's returning footsteps sounded. He looked at Dawlish with an expansive grin.

'He showed the cleanest pair of heels I've ever seen,' he said. 'I simply can't believe that it happened, Pat. There were three policemen outside, in addition to Trivett.'

Dawlish's answering grin was as wide.

'Trivett meant him to have another chance to get away, and Penrose is a strong-minded man.'

Farningham gaped.

'Trivett——'

'I knew that he was going to play ball when he didn't hand-cuff Penrose as they went out,' Dawlish said. 'Trivett suspected what I was putting up to Penrose. Officially he couldn't countenance letting him stay free, but he has an uncomfortable feeling that I might be right, so he gave him the chance to get away.'

'He told his men to fire!'

'Shooting at a running man on even such a glorious night as this isn't easy,' said Dawlish. 'Oh, Trivett meant him to get away if he had the guts to try it. Now we're back where we started, except that we've some very curious information. I'll tell you all about it later,' he added. 'I must get back to the flat. Will you do something for me?'

'If I can,' said Farningham.

'In an hour's time, telephone my Uncle Jeremiah at Basing-stoke,' said Dawlish, 'and give him an inkling of what to expect. Also ask him to make sure that whoever turns up doesn't get away until I've rolled up; but, of course, mention no names. All clear?'

'Yes. But surely you can tell me a *little* more!'

'Later,' said Dawlish firmly.

As he walked to the nearest station he was followed, as he expected to be.

Munk, for it was he, stuck doggedly behind him until he reached his flat.

Dawlish called out to him as he opened the street door, and was smiling when he went upstairs, where Tim and Felicity were waiting.

He stood back to watch their faces as he delivered his bombshell with great gusto.

'Penrose has escaped!'

'Penrose!' exclaimed Tim.

'Now what have you been doing?' demanded Felicity, but there was a gleam in her eyes.

'It wasn't really my idea,' said Dawlish, 'but Mr. Bloom's.'

He talked for almost half an hour, telling the story from Penrose's angle and not his own, and leading up to the climax with his own idea of Trivett's complicity. Then he sat back, awaiting comments. None came for some time, then Felicity said:

'What do you make of this trade mark, Pat?'

'It's the key to our problem,' Dawlish said thoughtfully. 'Penrose knows that it's important and thinks that one of the Haling firm is in danger; it's curious that he's prepared to sacrifice his life rather than to tell what he knows, don't you think?'

'It's unbelievable!' said Tim.

'You didn't hear him say it,' said Dawlish soberly. 'He sounded absolutely authentic, though I think he knows far more about the trade mark and the mystery than he's yet admitted. The self-sacrifice might be a pose, but it might also be the outcome of a situation to which he has resigned himself.'

'What are you going to do?' asked Felicity.

'Until we know that he's arrived safely, nothing,' said Dawlish, 'except take a nap, as I shall soon be going out again.'

It was characteristic of Dawlish to fall asleep within five minutes.

He slept for three hours.

Felicity was dozing in an easy-chair when the telephone bell rang, and in a few seconds she was talking to Farningham.

Before she finished, Dawlish was standing in the doorway of the room, watching her hopefully.

Sir Jeremiah Pinkerton was a small, red-faced and irascible gentleman, a Justice of the Peace, a bachelor, a wealthy man and something of an eccentric. In addition, he was an uncle of Patrick Dawlish. Several years before there had been a burglary at the country home of Sir Jeremiah, when Dawlish had been staying there. He had interfered, and it had started him on what his friends called, ironically, his career. There he had first met Trivett and Munk; there he had first discovered that he had a nose for mystery.

The old man now lived at Arum Cottage, near Basingstoke, where he was looked after by a man and wife and by them, according to his relatives, thoroughly spoiled.

It was his habit to sit in his study, reading, until the small hours, and Farningham's telephone call did not disturb him. At first he pretended not to recognise Farningham's name, although he knew it well; then he declared that he would take part in no nonsensical business in which his irresponsible nephew might be involved. Next he said that if anyone who had no right to his liberty arrived at Arum Cottage he would immediately turn him over to the police; and finally he told Farningham not to be an ass; for Farningham had protested rather anxiously.

That was after half-past eight.

It was the habit of the servants to retire to their own rooms after dinner; Pinkerton did not think that either of them were likely to be disturbed, but he took the trouble to go along to tell them that he was expecting a friend to pay a late call, and that he would answer the bell.

Then he returned to his room and began to read.

A little after one o'clock, the front doorbell rang.

Sir Jeremiah carefully shut his book, turned out the hall light and opened the door.

By the light of the stairs he could see the figure of a man standing there.

'Major Dawlish——'

'Come in.'

When the door was closed Sir Jeremiah switched on the light. He saw the pale face and dishevelled clothes of the escaped prisoner.

He beamed.

'*Now* what's the young fool been up to?'

Without waiting for an answer he led the way to the study.

'Come along, my boy, come along! You want a drink I know! Friends of my irresponsible nephew always do.' He tottered to his desk and took out a bottle of whisky.

'Say when!'

'I—er—I'm very grateful, sir,' said Penrose, 'but I would rather have a cup of tea, if you could possibly arrange it.'

Pinkerton looked up with a start.

'Tea!'

'Yes, I——'

'Dammit, man, why?'

'I—I'm practically a teetotaller,' Penrose burst out.

'A blue ribbon!' gasped Pinkerton. 'Dammit man, you must be an impostor!'

'I assure you——' Penrose was alarmed.

'You must be! Patrick Dawlish never made a friend of a teetotaller yet! Wait a minute, though—I think he married one. Married one without asking my permission, too. I was away at the time, he couldn't even get in touch with me. But *is* she a teetotaller, or just a moderate drinker, now?' He screwed up his face and then burst into a cackle. 'All right, my boy, all right! Tea it shall be. Hungry?'

'I am, rather,' admitted Penrose.

'I'll see what I can find,' said Pinkerton. 'I shall get rapped over the knuckles in the morning for nosing about the larder—never let yourself be victimised by a woman, my boy, never take the risk! When did you last eat?'

'At twelve o'clock,' said Penrose.

'Twelve? An hour ago?'

'No—noon.' Penrose looked at Pinkerton as if unable to grasp the fact that this old man was a connection of Dawlish's. 'Prison food isn't bad, but——'

'*Prison!*' gasped Pinkerton.

Penrose stared. 'Surely Major Dawlish——'

'The—utter—fool!' squeaked Sir Jeremiah, 'getting *me* to harbour an escaped felon! That is what you are, don't deny it! An escaped felon! And I am a Justice of the Peace! Confound his impudence! What was your crime?'

'I—I'm awaiting trial,' said Penrose weakly.

'Trial! What for?'

'M-murder,' gasped Penrose.

Sir Jeremiah stared at him from narrowed eyes, nodded his head several times and then reached the kitchen. Without another word he collected bread, butter, cheese, the remains of a rabbit pie, and put them on the table. Then he plugged in a kettle.

'Eat, while I go and find out what that young upstart is thinking of!' He tottered to the door and then turned abruptly: 'I might turn you out in the morning, but you can stay here tonight. Enjoy your food!'

He went to telephone Farningham, and Farningham put in the call to Dawlish.

Dawlish left the flat a little after two o'clock, and walked to his garage. Munk or another man followed him. Dawlish took out his Bentley, for which he had enough petrol for the run to Basingstoke and back, and returned to Brook Street, where he picked up Felicity and Tim. Tim had telephoned Creem and Napier telling them to set out on the Basingstoke road in an hour's time and to keep a sharp look-out.

The police had not expected Dawlish to leave by car, and although the man who relieved Munk telephoned an urgent S.O.S. immediately to the Yard, it was too late to follow Dawlish.

Driving with a gay abandon, he had not long left London before he became aware of the fact that a vehicle was behind him. It was not a car but a tradesman's van, which in spite of the Bentley's seventy miles an hour, maintained a remarkable speed.

CHAPTER SEVENTEEN

ROADSIDE INCIDENT

THEY were on the flat stretch of road between Blackwater and Camberley when Dawlish leaned back to speak to Tim.

'Do you feel like a deed of heroism?' he asked.

'No,' said Tim promptly. 'What particular deed?'

'When we're off this stretch of flat there are one or two twists and turns in the road,' said Dawlish. 'If I slow down at one of them, will you hop off?'

'And walk the rest of the way?' asked Tim coldly.

'Ass. I'll stop the van that's following us. Whoever is in it will think that there is no threat from the rear. Then you arrive and cause panic. Will do?'

'All right, it's worth a try,' said Tim resignedly. 'Say when.'

Felicity said: 'It might be an innocent van, Pat.'

'I'll lay you ten to one that it belongs to Haling & Haling. There's one thing we weren't told about,' said Dawlish sanctimoniously, 'and that is that some of their vans have superchargers. This one certainly has, or it couldn't have stood the pace. Stand by, Tim!'

There was a decline in the flat stretch of road, ending in a sharp bend. It was natural enough that he should slow down. The hedge on the side of the road hid the Bentley from the driver of the van. Tim was up and over the side in a flash, and his 'Okay' floated back to them a second or two later.

Felicity looked back nervously.

Dawlish was always unpredictable, and she did not know what he planned to do, nor what surprise element the men in the van would spring.

'Hold tight,' Dawlish warned her suddenly.

She clutched the door, and a moment later he braked, swinging the wheel to the right. The Bentley slewed across the road. Dawlish righted it, but the engine had stalled; there was no room for the van to pass.

Dawlish said: 'Stay here, Fel.' He climbed out of the car, his right hand in his pocket about a gun, carried a torch in his left. He played the powerful beam on the van, which came to a standstill, its brakes squealing, only a few feet away.

Four men were climbing from the back.

One would not have surprised Dawlish, or even two, but four were a different matter. They were quickly joined by the driver, who appeared to be in charge, and the man who had been sitting beside him.

Dawlish called out:

'Lend a hand, there, will you?'

It amused Dawlish that the six men should advance in a bunch. Probably they had been warned that he could throw his weight about effectively, for there was no doubt that they were nervous.

'I skidded, but it's nothing much.' He looked up and seemed to notice how many men there were for the first time. 'By George, just the gang for this job! Set to, my hearties, overtime rates!'

He waved his torch in a haphazard arc, which gave him the glimpse he wanted. The name painted on the side of the van was Haling & Haling. None of the men spoke; they seemed nonplussed by Dawlish's reception.

The driver came a step in front of his party. He too seemed apprehensive.

'Are you Dawlish?'

'As a matter of fact I am. Look here, what's on your mind?' asked Dawlish.

He could not make out the driver's features, but he could see the five pale blurs of the faces of the other men. They were grouped in a half-circle and three of them had their hands in their pockets. Their indecision puzzled him.

The driver said: 'Where's Penrose?'

For a single moment exultation flooded Dawlish. He had achieved what he had set out to do; they were after Penrose, and it could only be because the accused man was the weak chink in their armour. He was glad that it was dark, and his elated expression was invisible, but it passed quickly, he prepared to tackle the present situation. Six men, all presumably armed, made the odds unpleasantly heavy.

'Penrose?' he echoed, as if puzzled.

'Yes, Penrose. Where is he?'

'Didn't he escape?' asked Dawlish vaguely.

'Don't play the fool with us! You know he escaped, you helped him to!'

'Now that isn't true,' said Dawlish, 'I chased after him, but I can't even be sure that he was Penrose because we didn't get very near each other. I don't know where he is now, I'm afraid.'

The driver appeared to be undecided. This puzzled Dawlish. Then he caught a glimpse of one of the men looking over his shoulder.

Perhaps Bloom was on the way here. If they were only stalling, until he arrived, it would explain their attitude.

From a long way off there came the high-powered hum of a car. Dawlish hoped that the driver would take the precaution of putting a man on the other side of the bend, to make sure that there was no crash. Hardly was the thought in his mind than the driver gave instructions and a man walked along the road, his footsteps loud and clear.

It was a bizarre situation.

Dawlish had been half-prepared for rough treatment, perhaps for shooting first and questions afterwards; he had taken a chance, and it had come off, but he did not know a great deal more than he had before. They were playing for time just as he was.

The hum of the oncoming car drew nearer.

The car, a Hillman saloon, half-turned the corner, and began to slow down. It slid past the van and came to a halt. An authoritative voice called sharply:

'Get that car out of the ditch, you fools!'

The men sprang to life. Only the driver waited with Dawlish, and now he made no secret of the fact that he had a gun. The other five men managed to lift the Bentley's wheel clear, and then pushed the big car to the side of the road. The driver of the van stood covering Dawlish.

There was no sign of Tim.

'Now get the van nearer the edge,' snapped the man from the Hillman.

Was it Bloom?

Dawlish tried to see through the darkness, but could not distinguish the face or figure of the newcomer; all he knew was that he was used to command, that the others had expected him and that he was in a foul temper.

At last the cars were placed as he wanted them and the man in the Hillman climbed out.

Dawlish saw at once that he was enormously fat, and that he could not, by any chance, be Haling in disguise.

'Take Dawlish to the van,' he said, 'and leave the woman here.'

Dawlish hesitated, but saw no point in objecting. Tim was keeping well out of sight and none of the others had any idea that he was at hand. If any emergency developed while he was in the van, Tim would look after Felicity. The risk was obviously great, yet he was not unduly perturbed as he walked to the back of the van, the fat man following, breathing heavily.

Dawlish schooled himself to show no surprise.

The inside of the van was furnished with a desk and filing cabinets. There was a small wireless transmitting set of military pattern, over which a man with earphones was crouching. He was a brown-faced little fellow, whose beady eyes turned momentarily to Dawlish. Another man, ludicrously small in comparison to Bloom, held a torch.

For this *was* Bloom. Of that, Dawlish had no doubt at all.

The van started to move.

'Don't get worked up, Dawlish,' the fat man advised him, 'we're only going off the road so that we won't be noticed by passing traffic. You and your wife won't be hurt if you act sensibly.'

Dawlish said nothing.

Bloom, who had been watching Dawlish closely, took out a cigar case and proffered it.

'I'd rather have a pipe,' said Dawlish.

'Please yourself.' Bloom cut the end off a cigar and lit it. Dawlish slowly filled his pipe. Bloom waited until that was drawing well, before he spoke again. 'Well, Dawlish, I suppose you know what I want?'

'From what I gathered from those bright specimens outside, you want Penrose,' said Dawlish.

'Yes. Where is he?'

'I don't know.'

'You took him away.'

'I tried to, but he wouldn't play,' said Dawlish. 'Not that it matters now, one way or the other.'

'What do you mean?' demanded Bloom sharply. 'When you interfered with my plans at Brixton and chased after Penrose, you minded plenty. What were you doing at the prison, any-way?'

'I was going to see Penrose,' said Dawlish. 'I had managed to get permission from the police in a forlorn hope to make them see sense,' he went on. 'I ought to have known better, of course.'

'Are you implying that you are no longer working with the police?'

Dawlish shrugged.

'Why this remarkable *volte-face*?' demanded Bloom.

Dawlish grinned. 'Your very existence is doubted!'

'There are limits even to what I'll take from the authorities,' he went on soberly, 'and those limits have been passed. If you are worried about what I'm going to do next, forget it. I'm leaving London for a few days, and letting the police stew in their own juice.'

'Why choose such an unusual hour?'

'Because I've no right to my petrol, and it's easier to slip away from the police after dark.'

The fat man regarded Dawlish with expressionless eyes.

'I don't believe you, Dawlish. I think you are going to see Penrose. I think this talk of a quarrel between you and the police is eye-wash, and that someone thought it an excellent way to pull the wool over my eyes. It isn't going to succeed. I think you hoped that you would force this interview by what you have done. You have succeeded there, but it will afford you no satis-faction. I want to know where Penrose is.'

He took an automatic pistol from his pocket and laid it on the desk; and at the same moment the thin man moved up to Dawlish and began to go through his pockets.

CHAPTER EIGHTEEN

BLOOM THREATENS

DAWLISH'S automatic and his knife, which had many gadgets and of which he was very fond, were put on the desk. Dawlish made no effort to prevent himself from being searched.

'You take this very calmly,' Bloom said.

'I am placid by nature,' said Dawlish amiably.

'I have heard that you are a remarkable man, and I am beginning to agree,' said Bloom. 'You are aware, aren't you, that your wife is outside and that it will depend entirely on the result of this interview whether you ever see her again.'

'Oh,' said Dawlish. 'Threats?'

The fat man shrugged.

'I dislike using them, but with you something of the kind is necessary. You and your wife are completely in my hands.'

'I see.'

'Don't forget it,' said Bloom. 'Before we go on to more important things, I would like to know how you learned that I sometimes worked with colleagues at Pymm Place.'

Dawlish lowered his eyes.

Until that moment he had believed that Bloom had deliberately lured him to Pymm Place, although there had been times when he had wondered what had possessed the man to do it. Now he knew that the man who had called himself Blossom was *not* Bloom. In a flash, he realised that someone working with Bloom had wanted him to see the Lampleys, and had deliberately given him the clue which had helped so much.

'Well?' snapped Bloom.

'I have my methods,' said Dawlish airily. 'I've been interested in this business for some time, Bloom, mainly because I knew Haling & Haling were helping Penrose and I thought I might look round. I wasn't grateful for your trick with the trap,' he added abruptly.

'That was prepared when you were seen near Wimbledon,' said Bloom. 'So it wasn't Smythe who told you?'

'No,' said Dawlish. 'He told me a lot, but he boasted in his sleep—his dying sleep—that he had kept one thing back. He tried hard, Bloom, you shouldn't have killed him.'

'Whenever I think it necessary to kill, I shall kill,' said Bloom coldly, 'and I shall not hesitate. I am puzzled,' he admitted unexpectedly. 'What possessed you to bring your wife from London without an escort? We followed you carefully. Not even the police did that, although the sergeant on duty outside your flat telephoned to Scotland Yard and reported your sudden departure.'

'You're very thorough,' murmured Dawlish.

'I am efficient,' said Bloom. 'There is for instance, little or no risk in talking to you like this. Even if you have made some preparations to meet an emergency, those preparations will be useless. I know what I am doing, and I know what I want. I am not convinced by the smokescreen of publicity which you have put out. I do not believe that you are no longer working with the police. I believe you know where Penrose is. In five minutes I shall also know, or else you will be going through a most unpleasant experience.'

'I see,' repeated Dawlish.

He was beginning to dislike Bloom intensely. His dispassionate manner was disquieting; there was no bluster, only a quiet, unnerving confidence that he would get what he wanted. Dawlish wished that Felicity were here with him and for the first time began to wonder whether Tim's help would be effective.

Nearly three-quarters of an hour had passed from the time he had dropped Tim; Napier and Creem were probably near Staines, about twelve miles away.

'Now, Dawlish,' Bloom said patiently, 'where is Penrose?'

'I have no idea,' said Dawlish.

'You are lying!'

'Now you're being childish,' said Dawlish. 'There is nothing I can do about that. I don't know where Penrose is. As a matter of fact, Penrose is the bone over which the police and I finally quarrelled, but as you don't believe that either, what's the point in talking about it?'

'You are very obstinate,' said Bloom.

'As a matter of fact I'm tired out,' said Dawlish. 'I haven't had much rest these last few days, you've kept me too fully occupied!'

'Two of those five minutes have gone,' said Bloom, his voice expressionless.

'Well, I can't tell you what I don't know,' said Dawlish.

Silence fell. He could hear a clock ticking but he could not see the clock itself. He stared into Bloom's narrowed eyes, wishing he knew how far the man would go.

The night was very quiet; only an occasional footstep or a muffled sneeze disturbed it.

Bloom stirred at last.

'Fetch Mrs. Dawlish,' he said, without moving his head.

A torch was shone on Dawlish while the other light was switched off. In an eerie quiet, the thin man pushed the tarpaulin aside and went down the steps. The sound of footsteps followed, faded and then came nearer; Dawlish recognised Felicity's.

The tarpaulin was drawn again and the light switched on.

Bloom turned to look at her.

'Where is your husband going?' he demanded in the same even voice.

'I don't think he knows,' said Felicity.

'Mrs. Dawlish, I have already warned him of the consequences of being obstinate. Don't make the mistake of thinking that you are not in danger. Where is he going?'

Felicity glanced at Dawlish. There was a suggestion of: 'now-look-what-you've-done' attitude in her manner.

'He got me up in the middle of the night, said that he was tired of London and the police, and—well, I rather expected to get as far as Salisbury before he stopped,' Felicity said. 'We have some friends there.'

Obviously Bloom was nonplussed.

'Where is Penrose?' he snapped.

'How on earth should I know?' asked Felicity.

'You knew that he had escaped from prison?'

'Yes,' she said, 'Pat did tell me that, but he's been like a bear with a sore head since he got home this evening, and I've hardly had a word out of him.' The reproach remained, and Dawlish could have hugged her; she had found the one reasonable way to avoid answering questions which Bloom might put.

Bloom pushed his chair back and stood up.

'I want you both to understand that I am not being deceived,' he said, 'and that unless you tell me the whole truth I shall make things extremely painful for you. Dawlish, if you have in fact quarrelled with the police, there is no point in refusing to tell me where Penrose is.'

'It isn't a case of refusal,' said Dawlish, 'I just don't know.'

Bloom stared at him fixedly for several seconds, and then turned and raised a hand to the thin man who, until then, had been standing still at the back of the van. At the gesture from Bloom he moved across to Felicity, spun her round and slapped her face. The blow was not hard, although it was enough to send her reeling against the opposite side of the van. The thin man grabbed her arm and pulled her upright again. Then he struck her on the other cheek. She fell against Dawlish, who put a hand out to catch her.

Bloom held the gun poised.

The thin man stepped to Felicity to pull her from Dawlish; Dawlish lifted her from her feet with one hand and swept the other round, the fist clenched. He caught the thin man just beneath the jaw, and lifted him inches off the ground. The report of the blow echoed loudly, and the man's teeth snapped together; he slumped down to the floor, where he lay inert.

Bloom tightened his grip on the gun; the radio operator took an automatic from his pocket and covered Dawlish. The big man lifted his wife and carried her to one of the chairs by the filing cabinets; then turned to look at Bloom.

'That was a mistake,' he said, 'I had just decided to be through with this business. It had nothing to do with me and as the police played the fool it wasn't worth going on. Now you've given me a personal interest.'

Bloom said: 'Are you *sane*, Dawlish?'

'People have doubted it,' admitted Dawlish. 'If I were you I would be very wary of maniacs, they're quite unpredictable. And if you think you're frightening me with those guns, think again.' There was an edge to his voice. 'The next time you or any of your men touch my wife, I'll really get mad.'

Bloom drew in his breath.

'Dawlish, you don't seem to realise——'

'I realise that I actively dislike you,' said Dawlish. 'Listen to me, Bloom. Do you think I'm fool enough to come out here, knowing that you're so interested in me, without making sure that I'm well guarded? Your men didn't *see* anyone following me—of course they didn't, because I wasn't followed, but my friends came ahead. You're not sitting as pretty as you think you are.'

'*No*-one can help you,' Bloom said.

'I've heard that so often that it no longer troubles me,' said Dawlish. 'It's time you grew up, Bloom.' He took his pipe from his lips and tapped it out in an ash-tray on the desk. Then he slipped it into his pocket. He made no effort to get at his own gun nor to knock Bloom's aside; he seemed completely oblivious of the threat of the automatics, and he glanced at Felicity again. She had recovered a little, but still looked dazed.

He had no idea what would happen next.

Bloom believed that he could lead the way to Penrose, and while the fat man continued to think so he would not do Dawlish any fatal injury; but he might try to persuade Dawlish to talk by tormenting Felicity. The question was, how far could Dawlish safely carry his bluff and what chance had Tim of turning the tables?

Bloom seemed to be in two minds.

The van was very quiet. Odd sounds came from outside, but there was no hint of alarm, no suggestion that Tim had been discovered; it was surprising how much depended on Tim.

A car hummed along the road, and went past; it was the first one he had heard. It was the forerunner of a line of heavy army vehicles on the inevitable trek south.

The convoy passed out of earshot; another solitary car went by and the noise of its engine faded.

'We aren't getting very far, are we?' asked Dawlish.

Bloom said: 'Why did you want to see Penrose?'

'A forlorn hope,' said Dawlish conversationally. 'It's mere routine to try everything, however long the shot.' He sounded rueful. 'If the police hadn't been such stubborn fools——' he shrugged his shoulders. 'Until your friends came up this evening I was prepared to be finished with the whole business. I don't get much leave and I don't see the point of wasting my time if I'm not wanted. The police think that they have the right man in Penrose, and they would have been quite happy to have convicted him but for your remarkable mistake.'

'Mistake?' snapped Bloom.

'Yes—the rescue of Penrose,' said Dawlish. 'It convinced them at long last that there is more behind this business than there appeared to be at first. *I* saw it pretty early,' he added with a grin. 'After all, the little sign you use is queer, isn't it? And on both girls——'

'What sign?' inquired Bloom.

'The circle within a star,' said Dawlish, 'don't tell me you don't know about it!'

'So you're on to that,' said Bloom softly. 'Dawlish, I was beginning to think that I might let you go and be rid of a nuisance. Now—no, I don't believe that you're going to drop out. You may have offended the police, but it wouldn't be in character for you to stop at this point. You were going to see Penrose, but I shall make that impossible.'

'That will be clever of you,' said Dawlish.

'Not so clever,' said Bloom. 'I shall leave your bodies by the side of your own car, it will look as if you were going at high speed and skidded.' There was no smile on his face, only dead earnestness; he meant to do it. 'I'll give you one more chance, Dawlish, to tell me where you are meeting Penrose. You have been a great nuisance already, and you will become a worse one if I don't act decisively.'

Dawlish said: 'I suppose another murder or two won't really trouble you, will it?'

Suddenly Felicity screamed!

It was the only way to summon Tim, the only way to tell him that the moment for his attempt at rescue had arrived, but heavy on Dawlish's mind there was the dark thought of the six armed men.

The thin man hurried to Felicity with an arm upraised—at the same time the hum of a car became clearly audible.

CHAPTER NINETEEN

NEW ARRIVALS

THE car slowed sown.

Inside the van there was utter silence. Felicity was staring wide-eyed at the man in front of her, while Dawlish and Bloom eyed each other, Bloom still clutching the gun. The car came to a standstill and the engine was switched off; then, suddenly, there came the sound of a shot.

'The fools!' Bloom snapped.

He jumped up. Dawlish was now nearer to his own gun, but not near enough to take chances.

Two more shots followed; footsteps were confused and men were shouting. Suddenly the tarpaulin was thrust aside and the van driver jumped in. He paused for breath, and then gasped:

'Guv'nor, there's some men——'

He pitched forward into the van, and for a moment all was confusion; then Dawlish arose with the automatic in his hand. The shooting outside increased in intensity, but he drowned it with a bellow.

'All right, there!'

Bloom, gradually recovering his balance, still held his gun, but Dawlish had the advantage. Nothing could have happened more suddenly, or taken Bloom more completely by surprise. His lips were parted and he was breathing heavily.

Tim Jeremy thrust the tarpaulin aside and jumped in.

'Why, hallo!' said Dawlish, laughing. 'So the others arrived?'

'I saw the car coming and stood in the road to attract their attention,' said Tim in high good-humour. He was now facing the back of the van and his gun was pointing towards it. 'I think they'll be able to look after the half-dozen nitwits outside, don't you?'

'Five,' corrected Dawlish, 'you dealt with one.'

He stepped to Bloom's side, took the gun out of his hand and passed it to Felicity.

'What is called the Turning of the Tables!' He beamed. 'How does it feel, Bloom?'

'Dawlish——'

'Don't tell me that I won't get away with it,' said Dawlish, 'it begins to pall.'

Bloom said: 'Dawlish, all this shooting will have attracted attention!'

'I realised that,' said Dawlish. 'Hallo, now what?'

He broke off at the sound of the deep throbbing note of the Bentley's engine. Leaping to the ground he saw the headlights as the Bentley gathered speed and was driven south. Another

116

car followed, presumably the Hillman. There were three shots, and he could just make out the figures of two men standing in the road.

He called out: 'Ahoy, there!'

'The perishers pinched the cars,' said Creem in a disgusted voice. He held the limp body of an unconscious man, which he bundled unceremoniously into the van.

'He's all we could get,' said Napier, his drawling voice filled with regret. 'We didn't realise that two cars were along the road, Pat. They went for them as soon as we started shooting, and —well, that's that.' He shrugged his shoulders and jumped up into the van. Creem followed him, and Dawlish dropped the tarpaulin.

Napier and Creem looked at Bloom with evident surprise and pleasure, and Creem began to smile.

'Not bad, not bad at all. Is it an early Bloom or a late Blossom?'

'Just a minute,' said Dawlish hiding a grin. 'What car did you bring?'

'Nat's Lancia.'

'It'll be a bit of a squeeze,' said Dawlish, 'but Bloom is going with us to Uncle Jerry. The others can stay here.' He looked about for some rope. In less than five minutes the thin man, the radio-operator and the van-driver were neatly trussed up, and Dawlish had jumped down to the ground. He led the way towards the Lancia. Bloom followed, with Napier just behind him. Felicity, Tim and Creem brought up the rear.

Dawlish looked at the car in the light of his torch, and then slowly shook his head.

'No can do,' he said. 'Someone will have to stay behind. Not a bad idea, really. He can drive the van with the prisoners to Camberley police station, and then we can telephone the Yard and give vent to a little discreet crowing! The only thing he mustn't do is to say where we have gone. Let's toss for it.'

Solemnly the three of them placed coins on their hands; the odd man was to stay with the van. Tim uncovered his first; it was heads. Napier followed; it was heads. Creem groaned, and uncovered his; it was tails.

Regretfully he turned to the van. By then several small lights were showing in the distance and Dawlish imagined that someone had heard the shooting and would soon be approaching. He hustled Bloom into the back of the car with Napier, while he himself took the wheel with Felicity and Tim beside him.

The lamps drew nearer and voices were raised, but Dawlish let in the clutch and started off.

Sir Jeremiah Pinkerton was nodding in an easy-chair. Penrose was sound asleep. The old man stirred when a clock struck five, and a few minutes afterwards sat bolt upright, for the front doorbell was ringing.

Penrose grunted in his sleep.

Pinkerton glanced at him, then hurried to open the door. Dawlish, Felicity and Bloom came in quickly; Napier was still in the car, keeping watch in case they had been followed.

Sir Jeremiah struck a dramatic attitude.

'Patrick, what have you been up to now?'

'Nothing much,' said Dawlish. 'You know Tim and Felicity, don't you?'

'Of course I do,' said Pinkerton, sinking comfortably back to his normal height. 'I haven't forgiven you for getting married without me, but I won't hold it against you!' He pecked Felicity's cheek. 'I'll welcome you afterwards, my dear, I want to know what all this remarkable fuss is about first!'

He looked at Bloom, who seemed to fill the hall.

The fat man had sat in sullen silence throughout the journey, and he was still sullen.

'Has the other man arrived?' Dawlish asked.

He did not need an answer, for Penrose, risen from sleep, stood on the threshold.

Bloom caught sight of him.

He drew in a deep breath, and swung round on Dawlish. Penrose stared at him as if bewildered.

Dawlish said: 'Yes, I knew where Penrose was, Bloom.'

'What *is* this all about?' asked Pinkerton irritably.

'You shall have the whole story in good time,' Dawlish promised him. 'Just now there's something to be done.' He manoeuvred them all into the study, then stood back and confronted Bloom.

'Bloom, I want to know why you arranged to release Penrose. If you haven't told me in sixty seconds, you'll get hurt.'

Bloom opened his mouth to speak, but closed it again.

'So *this* is Bloom!' exclaimed Penrose.

'This is the gentleman,' said Dawlish, his voice harsh, 'and he is going to talk freely or pay for his silence.'

Bloom was breathing even more heavily. Dawlish suddenly shot out his right hand towards him.

Penrose muttered: 'Dawlish, you mustn't——'

'Don't talk like a fool!' snapped Dawlish roughly, 'he has been responsible for killing at least four people and for trying to get you convicted for a murder which you say you haven't done. Bloom——'

Bloom gasped: 'All right, Dawlish, all right!'

'You'd better make it all right,' said Dawlish.

There was a moment's pause before Bloom began to speak in a low-pitched, hesitating voice. Penrose stared at him as if fascinated, and the others were almost as tense.

'I wanted to get Penrose because—there was a danger that he might break up my organisation,' Bloom said.

'I couldn't,' exclaimed Penrose, 'I didn't know it existed!'

'You know that only a few people could use that sign,' said Bloom. The words seemed dragged from him. 'Everything stood or fell by that sign. Once it was clear that the police were interested in it there was always the danger that you would recognise its origin—and make a statement which would prove disastrous.' He was gasping for breath, now, and there was a beading of perspiration on his forehead.

Dawlish watched him curiously, for his behaviour was out of character, and, to him, this scene did not ring quite true.

He said: 'Did the sign mean so much?'

'Yes,' admitted Bloom. 'Yes, it——' he broke off.

'I don't want to hurt you,' said Dawlish, 'but I shall get really rough if you're much longer.'

'The sign—meant everything,' Bloom said. 'We used it as—as a code.'

'That still doesn't explain how Penrose could have given anything away,' said Dawlish.

Bloom gasped: 'He could have named all the people who knew about it in the first place, and——'

He broke off, because Penrose uttered a sharp exclamation. The younger man's face was drained of its colour, and he was staring at Dawlish.

'You see?' he said, with a helpless note in his voice. 'One of the company——' he broke off in turn, and it was some time

119

before he went on slowly: 'One of the company is in this business. I knew that only a member of the company could have authorised the use of the vans, it couldn't have been done altogether by outsiders.'

'It's beginning to look like that,' Dawlish said, turning again to Bloom. 'So you wanted to prevent Penrose from saying anything to the police which might incriminate one of the partners of Haling & Haling. But it was you who put Penrose in the hands of the police in the first place.'

Bloom had lost every vestige of colour.

'I didn't know who Penrose was until afterwards. I didn't know that he might have seen the sign on the shoulders of the two girls, that's where everything began to go wrong. When I learned who Penrose was——' he stopped again and licked his lips.

'Well, well!' exclaimed Dawlish, 'it's been quite a chapter of misunderstandings, hasn't it? When you got Penrose out of Brixton, what did you intend to do with him?'

Bloom said: 'He——'

'Out with it!'

'We should have killed him and tried to make it look like suicide,' said Bloom. 'This is all your fault, damn you!' He swung round on Dawlish with a clenched hand shaking in front of his face. 'It's all your fault, if you'd kept out of it this would never have happened! I knew it from the first, I knew you were more likely than the police to find out what was behind it, but—*you won't find out!*'

Something seemed to possess the man. It might have been that the worst depth of fear had been plumbed, or that he now realised that he was not likely to get away and that nothing he said could make matters worse.

'So you don't think I'll find out,' Dawlish said.

'No one *knows* except me and two others,' Bloom snapped, 'and you won't find them, because if they don't hear that I'm safe after tonight, they will disappear. They may have to stop work for a few weeks, but they'll be able to take it up where I've left off!' He drew in his breath, and he gave the impression that he was about to burst into tears.

Felicity looked away, but Tim was looking at Dawlish with more than a hint of disgust in his expression.

Dawlish said: 'So they'll be able to take over, will they?'

'Yes, and nothing you can do will stop them, damn you!'

'Dear, dear,' exclaimed Dawlish. He was preoccupied by the astonishing change in Bloom's manner. This petulant defiance was remarkable; so was the fact that he had recovered from the initial shock in such a way. Earlier on, Dawlish had come to the conclusion that Bloom had been really frightened; now he was sure that the man was putting on an act.

Would it be wise to say so?

Dawlish decided against it.

'Nothing you can do——' began Bloom again, but Dawlish swung round and spoke to Penrose.

'Who else knew of this sign, or whatever you call it?'

'The Halings, Lampley, Arnold, the Manager and Warren, the secretary. The Transport Manager also knew—his name is Symes.'

'So two of these are in it with Bloom,' said Dawlish, thoughtfully. 'You thought they were, didn't you?'

'You know I did,' said Penrose. 'I can't believe——'

'You won't be able to catch them, I tell you,' said Bloom. 'As soon as they realise I'm not there to report, they'll disappear!'

'You said that before,' said Dawlish. 'They'll only disappear once, won't they?' He drew hard on his cigarette, and then grinned. 'All right, we'll see what does happen when you don't report. I rather think you're too optimistic, Bloom, they'll come a cropper in exactly the same way as you. The Haling brothers, Lampley, Warren, Arnold and Symes,' he repeated, as if to himself. 'Can I use the telephone, Uncle Jerry?'

The telephone was in the hall, as Sir Jeremiah Pinkerton refused to have one in his study.

Felicity followed Dawlish out.

'Pat, what do you make of it?'

'It's a very queer turn-out indeed,' said Dawlish thoughtfully. 'Did you notice the way Bloom changed?'

'Yes. Something seemed to make him more confident, and then he started shouting defiance.'

'Of course, he may have been seized with an idea, or I may have said something that told him I had the wrong end of the stick,' said Dawlish. 'He seems quite sure that we won't have any trouble in identifying the people working with him. It's very odd indeed, and the police might as well do some of the handling.' He lifted the receiver and put in the call, holding on until Scotland Yard answered. He was pleasantly surprised to find Trivett in.

CHAPTER TWENTY

THE DISAPPEARANCE OF THE DIRECTORS

'HALLO, Bill,' said Dawlish, heartily, 'what's got you up so early in the morning?'

Trivett did not sound amused.

'I hear that you've had some trouble at Camberley,' he said gruffly. 'I've just come in to take a report.'

'Well, Creem can tell you as much about that as I can, and you've got one of the Haling company's vans completely fitted up as a mobile office. A curious development. Its engine is supercharged, too. You see, it worked.'

'What worked?'

'The bait for Bloom,' said Dawlish patiently, 'I have just been talking to him.

'Is that true?' asked Trivett sharply.

'What makes you doubt it?' asked Dawlish. 'Yes, he's here, very much against his will. Apparently the executive staff of Haling & Haling are in the know, and two or three of the directors more deeply involved. Bloom thinks that they'll disappear when it's known that he's caught. You've got all the names, haven't you?'

'Of course.'

'Then I'd get after them if I were you,' said Dawlish. 'Haul 'em all in for questioning, and make sure that they can't slip away in a hurry. Will you fix that?'

'Yes. But if you're trying to put anything else over me——'

'Oh, grow up!' said Dawlish impatiently. 'I'm telling you what Bloom has said. He's here, in the flesh.'

'Where is "here"?'

'Arum Cottage, on the Newbury road from Basingstoke,' said Dawlish. 'I hope that we'll be safe, but I wouldn't swear that we aren't being watched. Tell whomever you send along to look out for corpses.'

'Must you be so flippant?' asked Trivett.

'To be saved from a sticky end in the nick of time is inclined to make one flippant,' said Dawlish. 'It's cheaper than fireworks. Has anything happened your end?'

'There are one or two things that might interest you,' said Trivett grudgingly, and Dawlish's attention quickened. 'The pseudo padre had a false set of papers, certifying that he came from Penrose's unit. He was a frequent visitor at the prison.'

'Was he, by George!'

'There's one other thing. The "padre" was a visitor to Smythe's flat.'

'By George, you've been busy!' exclaimed Dawlish.

'We aren't altogether useless,' said Trivett. 'Does any of this help you at all?'

'I think it does,' said Dawlish. 'Yes, I certainly think it does, Bill! Well, don't forget to send someone along.'

He rang off and contemplated the others thoughtfully.

Felicity said: 'Do you seriously think we'll be attacked?'

'It wouldn't surprise me,' said Dawlish. 'The Bentley and the Hillman are somewhere, you know. I think they might have been parked in a side road, and started after us when we passed. They've had plenty of time to send for help, too. Still, they were pretty timid, so we might be all right. It would be nice to know why Bloom travelled about the country in that van, but Trivett will be on to that by now. They should glean quite a lot from those filing cabinets. You must be pretty tired, what about going to bed?'

'I'll go when you do,' said Felicity.

'I was afraid of that,' admitted Dawlish.

He returned to the study, where he found the four men sitting in utter silence.

Tim opened one eye when Dawlish returned.

'Not a word has been said,' he declared.

'Astonishing. Well here's something to think about at least,' said Dawlish. 'The police are of this moment busily arresting all the directors and all the executive staff of Haling & Haling. A thought to crow over, eh, Bloom?'

Bloom drew in his breath.

'Dawlish——' Penrose began, only to turn his face away, as if the news had been the one final straw too many. Dawlish eyed him thoughtfully, and then shrugged his shoulders.

'We can now only wait. Are you expecting a rescue party, Bloom? Or are those weak-kneed gunmen of yours more likely to save their own precious skins?' When Bloom did not answer, he added: 'All right, we'll wait on events. Uncle Jerry, I think Felicity ought to go to bed for an hour or two, and forty winks wouldn't do you any harm.'

'*I'm* not tired,' declared Pinkerton stoutly. 'When are the police coming here?'

'Unless I misjudge Trivett he will send people from London rather than act from Basingstoke,' said Dawlish, 'but he might get the local people to send an advance guard to make sure we don't go away.' He grinned. 'I'm afraid you'll have to go back this time, Penrose, but you can rest happier—we're pretty near the truth, now. Bloom will admit that you were framed, don't worry about that.'

Penrose said: 'I would rather have died than cause trouble for the Halings!'

'Don't talk like a fool!' snapped Dawlish, 'it would have come out in the end. Now, Bloom—what's it all about?'

Bloom looked up briefly.

'I have nothing more to say.'

'You can at least tell me what is in the van,' said Dawlish, 'the police won't be long in finding out.'

'You fool!' said Bloom.

He uttered the words with such withering scorn that Dawlish was astonished. It brought a new tension into the room.

An interruption came from outside. It was a shrill whistle from Napier, followed by a thunderous banging on the front door. In such a situation Dawlish was at his best. He moved forward without a second's hesitation, throwing a word to Tim over his shoulder. Tim took out an automatic as Dawlish flung open the front door. Napier almost fell in.

Three men with guns were coming along the drive, clearly visible in the early morning light. A shot was fired and a bullet passed within an inch of Dawlish. Napier gasped out:

'They are at the back as well.'

'Of course they are,' said Dawlish. 'Upstairs, Tim! And Felicity, and you, Jerry. Bloom, I warn you that you're not going to be free for long. Penrose, come on!'

Penrose said: 'I don't understand——'

124

'There isn't time to understand,' snapped Dawlish. 'Bloom's rescue party has arrived.'

There was a crash as the front door flew open. Dawlish fired at the men who were crowding into the hall, and then took a grip on the banisters and pulled himself over, so that he was half-way up the stairs.

Bloom had appeared from the study and was shouting directions.

Dawlish reached the landing and swung round.

'Patrick!' howled Jeremiah, 'if you don't stop those men from wrecking my house, I—I——'

'You'd better send for the police,' said Dawlish, good-humouredly. 'They won't do much wrecking, though they've got what they want.'

By now the footsteps were heard in full retreat. The man on the drive suddenly began to run. A car engine started up, and then Dawlish heard the deep throbbing note of his Bentley. He looked out of the landing window rather sadly.

The two cars were some distance along the road and the men were hurrying towards them, Penrose and Bloom between them.

'Aren't you going to do anything?' demanded Napier.

'We will only waste bullets if we fire from here,' said Dawlish, 'they're too far away. They're moving too fast.'

'Confound it, you could try!'

'I would never have believed it of you,' declared Pinkerton, glaring at Dawlish. 'One would think that you *want* those two men to get away!'

'Yes, wouldn't one?' said Dawlish. 'As a matter of fact, I do.' He looked at the startled faces in front of him, and then chuckled. 'We couldn't have done much, you know. We might have put up a fight and we might even have stopped some of them from getting away, but we wouldn't have known the one important thing that we do know now.'

'What's that?' demanded Felicity.

'The rescue party want Penrose just as much as they want Bloom,' said Dawlish, 'in spite of the fact that Bloom knows that Penrose had told me a lot about the trade mark.' He lit a cigarette as he watched the Bentley being driven away. 'That's curious, isn't it? They took enormous risks to get Penrose into jail, and even greater risks to get him back. Had they only wanted to keep him quiet, they've had plenty of chances to kill him. The whole thing was phoney from the beginning.'

'This is too much for me,' said Napier.

'It's quite simple really,' said Dawlish, 'in a complicated way. Bloom intended all along to be caught, in order to get to Penrose—now we have to discover why.'

Felicity said: 'But Penrose has told us all he knows!'

'Has he?' asked Dawlish cryptically. 'It hardly looks like it. The fact remains that Bloom was prepared to go to fantastic lengths to get him, you know.'

'And you let him!' exclaimed Pinkerton.

'There wasn't any other way of finding out for certain what he wanted,' said Dawlish.

By now they were so tired that they decided to go to bed for what remained of the night.

Felicity was asleep within ten minutes.

Dawlish also dozed off, feeling certain that there would be no further alarms, at least until Trivett or the police arrived. His chief concern was for the van. He had warned both Creem and Trivett that it might hold some unpleasant secret. He remembered the withering 'you fool!' uttered by Bloom; from those two words he had judged that Bloom knew exactly what he was doing, and that the van was unlikely to deliver up any secrets to the police.

Immediately after receiving the telephone message from the Camberley police, Trivett had sent instructions that the van was not to be touched until he arrived to see it in person; that was as Dawlish had expected. The driver, the thin man and the radio-operator were lodged in cells at Camberley and the van itself was left in the yard outside the station.

Two or three constables on night duty looked at it from the window, but few people went near it. That was as well, because twenty minutes after the men had been taken out of it, and while Trivett was on his way from Scotland Yard, the van blew up.

Nat Creem was in the Inspector's office, drinking tea and eating sandwiches. The Inspector on duty was trying to find out what had been happening, and Creem was being charmingly vague.

The roar of the explosion made them both spring to their feet. The windows blew out, and heavy pieces of debris smashed into the walls of the police station. There were no serious injuries, however; but when Creem and the Inspector got outside, there was only a heap of wreckage, where the van had been, burning furiously.

The shock of the explosion had caught them all unaware, and the local Inspector was apparently more agitated by what the Yard man would say than by the damage.

Nat Creem was not. He remembered Dawlish's warning words, and wondered what else he knew or guessed.

CHAPTER TWENTY-ONE

S.O.S. FROM RENE LAMPLEY

TRIVETT was some time at Camberley. He did not telephone Arum Cottage, but arrived there by car a little after nine o'clock. Dawlish had slept for nearly three hours, and was wide awake when a maid announced that Trivett was downstairs.

He joined him in the study almost at once.

'Have you heard from Camberley?' Trivett asked abruptly.

'No.'

'The van was blown up.'

'That isn't going to surprise anyone, is it?' asked Dawlish. He smothered a yawn. 'Sorry.'

'You're not more tired than I am,' said Trivett, and then yawned himself. They grinned.

Dawlish was relieved to find the Yard man in a reasonably good mood.

'Well, Bloom rose to the bait, as indicated. He's a clever man and a good actor. He wanted Penrose very badly,' he added, and proceeded to go into some details with Trivett, who seemed surprised at nothing, and passed over the fact that Dawlish had made no effort to prevent Bloom and Penrose from being 'rescued'.

'Well, what's next?' asked Trivett peaceably.

'You're in a very amiable frame of mind, aren't you?' said Dawlish. 'As far as I can see, the next step is up to you. What about Haling & Haling directors?'

'We've made no detentions, but all the men are being watched. I left instructions for news to be telephoned to me here.'

'What kind of news?'

'Any attempt to get away,' said Trivett.

'If they haven't tried by now, they won't,' said Dawlish. 'Bloom might have lied, and I wouldn't be surprised if he had. You're in no great hurry, I suppose?'

'As a matter of fact I thought I might get a couple of hours sleep,' said Trivett.

'Sleep!' ejaculated Pinkerton, who had wandered in unobserved. 'Sleep! What on earth do you think this cottage is, a dormitory? All everyone has done is to sleep!' He stumped indignantly across the room, and then suggested that Trivett might like to lie down on a sofa in the lounge, as all the beds were occupied. Trivett chuckled, and Dawlish went upstairs to bath and shave.

He was glad of a brief respite.

He felt sure that Trivett wanted to stay at the cottage until news of some kind came from the Yard. He might even be waiting to be told what official attitude to adopt with Dawlish; the case had moved far from the time when Trivett had asked Dawlish to get leave, so as to help.

A call came through for Trivett just after eleven o'clock. He emerged from the lounge, rubbing his eyes, but he did not look tired the moment after he had lifted the receiver.

'*What?*' he shouted into the mouthpiece, and then more quietly: 'Are you sure? Why wasn't I told before? . . . All right, keep the others closely watched.'

'Others?' echoed Dawlish, who had come into the hall after him.

Trivett replaced the receiver, and then said slowly:

'George Haling and his brother are not at home. They disappeared before our men went to get them. The others are all at the factory now.'

'The Halings,' said Dawlish thoughtfully. 'Well, that's interesting, if nothing else. I suppose you've had no news of Lampley?'

'None at all,' said Trivett, who looked incensed. 'Why on earth they left it until now before telling me, I don't know!'

'What difference would it have made?' asked Dawlish. 'Forget your tantrums, Bill, and look at the evidence. Bloom said that his colleagues would disappear unless he reported at a certain time. He could not have reported very early, and the Halings have disappeared. There's a call out for them, I suppose?'

'Yes,' said Trivett. 'I thought you said that Bloom might have been lying.'

'So he might, but we can hardly take it for granted,' said Dawlish. 'He might have got away just too late, in which case we know two of the guilty members of the board of directors.' He lit another cigarette. 'Until you pick them up there isn't much we can do, but one fact sticks out a mile.'

'What's that?'

'We've got them worried.'

'And they've got me worried,' said Trivett gruffly. The news had disturbed him more than Dawlish thought it need have done. 'We still haven't the faintest idea of what they're doing. Going about the countryside by night with a mobile wireless and office—one would think they were on active service! If this had happened at the beginning of the war we would have thought them a highly organised gang of Nazi spies.'

'Yes, wouldn't we?' said Dawlish. 'Don't forget one possibility that also sticks out a mile, Bill.'

'What's that?'

'This particular van might have been fitted out to bluff us, and to make us think that we're on the look-out for similar vans and some kind of criminal conspiracy which demands such a means of transport and communication. Bloom knew that we would capture that van and made sure that we would not have a chance to examine it.'

'Confound it, that's too tortuous, even for these people!'

'Oh, I don't know,' said Dawlish.

Trivett looked at him thoughtfully.

'You know something, Pat, don't you?'

'Bill, I'll tell you one thing; I've given you every relevant fact, and any guess you make is as good as any of mine. I maintain that we've got them far more worried than they've got us.'

With that Trivett had to be satisfied.

Dawlish saw no point in staying at the cottage any longer; it had served its purpose, and after Felicity had come down they all had an early lunch and returned to London.

Trivett telephoned Scotland Yard from the flat, to find that nothing else had come in. As he went off, Creem arrived. The bulletin from the hospital was good, and Ted Beresford steadily improving. As this news was passed round there was a noticeable lightening of the atmosphere. They felt almost as if they were at the end of a successful chase; it was probably a false dawn, Felicity said, and they ought to rouse themselves out of the sense of complacency which had been induced by Dawlish's obvious satisfaction.

'Quite right, too,' said Dawlish, 'we oughtn't to be too cock-a-hoop, and yet I think we've really got them on the run. I also think that we shall hear from them quite soon.'

'From Bloom?' asked Tim, quickly.

'Indirectly, yes. I don't think he'll come in person,' said Dawlish. 'I do know this: we're going to handle whatever turns up on our own, and we'll tell Trivett about it afterwards. I think we've earned that much.'

Felicity made no comment; she was only too familiar with the ebullient moods which sometimes possessed Dawlish. While in the grip of one, he was likely to do much more foolish things than at normal times. There were moments when she was appalled at the lightness with which he took his life in his hands. Physical danger did not seem to worry him, and yet he often confessed after a particularly narrow shave that he had been scared stiff; Felicity was one of the few people who believed him.

They had tea at half-past four.

By then the waiting and inaction was beginning to pall. Napier and Creem were wrangling more or less good-humouredly, and Tim was acting as referee. Felicity was on edge, but trying to conceal it. They were all grouped round a large, low table, when the telephone rang.

Dawlish stretched out an arm and lifted the receiver.

'Dawlish speaking,' he said, and then his lips parted in a broad smile. 'Yes, Rene!' There was an almost triumphant note in his voice. 'Yes . . .' the triumph faded to be replaced by a look of concern. 'I might be able to do something,' he admitted, 'but you haven't been exactly helpful, you know.'

'I feel beastly about that,' said Rene Lampley. 'I—I'm sorry, but I think you will be able to help. I *daren't* tell the police.'

'All right,' said Dawlish. 'Where shall I meet you?'

'At Dr. Mordaunt's house, 18 Crescent Road, Wimbledon. He's the only man I feel that I can trust. You will come, won't you?'

'Yes, of course,' said Dawlish. 'And when you get to Mordaunt's house, don't leave for anyone but me. Good-bye.'

He replaced the receiver and took a long drink of tea.

'What did she want?' demanded Tim patiently.

Dawlish said: 'She's heard from Penrose, who says that he has managed to escape again and that he knows where her father is. He says also that if the police follow her she might regret it, and he has advised her to get in touch with me. That's in keeping with Penrose's general attitude, anyhow.'

Felicity said thoughtfully: 'Do you think Bloom has prompted this?'

'If you're asking me to guess, I would say that Bloom has let Penrose get away so that he can send this message to Rene,' said Dawlish. 'Fel, you'll stay here this time, won't you?'

'I suppose I'll have to,' said Felicity reluctantly.

'Napier will keep you company,' said Dawlish, 'it's his turn for sentry-go.'

There was no objection raised and, a few minutes later, Dawlish, Tim and Creem left the house. Dawlish had telephoned to a nearby garage and a taxi was waiting for them under the eye of a stationary policeman. Trivett was obviously taking precautions.

They reached 18 Crescent Road just after half-past five. A maid admitted them and led them to a pleasantly furnished drawing-room. Rene Lampley advanced with her hands outstretched. Dawlish looked at her with a smile.

'So you realise who your friends are at last!' he said.

'I—I hardly know what to say,' said Rene, her voice a little unsteady. 'Since father went it's been a nightmare! Now Charles and George Haling have disappeared and there's no way in which we can get in touch with them, except through Penrose. If I went to the police——'

'They would nab Penrose,' said Dawlish. 'You don't want them to get him, do you?'

'Of course not!'

'Why?' asked Dawlish.

'Does that matter now?' asked Rene urgently. 'We haven't any time to waste. If we're to find my father and to help

131

Alan——'

'*Alan?*' queried Dawlish softly.

The girl drew back. What little colour there was in her cheeks seemed to have drained away.

'I mean Penrose——'

'You mean Alan,' said Dawlish, his voice sharp. 'You lied when you said that you didn't know Penrose except by name, didn't you? Are you engaged to him?'

She looked so pale that he thought she would faint.

'Yes,' she said.

'I see,' said Dawlish more gently. 'Right from the beginning you've been afraid for him, haven't you? That's the explanation of much of your own and your father's reticence. You've been afraid that Penrose was a party to what was happening. That is why you and your father persuaded the Halings into trying to find out the secret of the vans without going to the police. That is the truth, isn't it?'

She said: 'Yes, it is.' Then her voice rose and she added swiftly: 'But he's got nothing to do with it, thank God! It's this man Bloom——'

'It's someone connected with Haling & Haling,' said Dawlish. 'Even if Penrose is clear, then you might have as great a shock. You won't like it if it should be George or Charles Haling, but supposing it should turn out to be your father?'

'It can't be!' she exclaimed. 'He's been kidnapped!'

'That might have been to put us off the track,' said Dawlish. 'There isn't any reasonable doubt that it's someone connected with the company.' He hesitated, and then asked in a low-pitched voice: 'How well do you know Dr. Mordaunt?'

'Dr. Mordaunt!' she exclaimed. 'I've known him ever since I can remember. *He's* not a criminal.'

'Can you be sure?' asked Dawlish.

'Oh, this is madness and we're losing precious time,' exclaimed Rene. 'You must see Penrose.'

'I'm trying to warn you that things might not turn out as you would like them to,' said Dawlish. 'All the people involved are your friends, aren't they?'

Tim shot Dawlish a reproachful glance; Creem looked as if he felt that Dawlish was piling it on a bit too much. Dawlish himself watched Rene steadily.

She said simply: 'Even if you're right, we must find Alan.'

'Of course. You want to come, I suppose?'

'Yes. I'll get my coat.' She turned and hurried out of the room, leaving the door open.

Dawlish turned urgently to the two men.

'One of you follow us, the other stay here. As soon as I've gone, telephone Trivett. Ask him to go to Number 11 Pymm Place. Tell him that he'll probably get what he wants there. Is that clear?'

'But——' began Tim.

'No time for buts,' said Dawlish. 'Ignore anything I say in her hearing. Tim, you'd better follow.' He drew away from the others as Rene came quickly down the stairs.

'That was fast work! You two had better get back to the flat, it's a one-man job this time.'

'Confound it——' protested Tim realistically.

'We haven't time to argue,' said Dawlish.

He led Rene out of the room and contrived to give the driver of the car the address which Rene passed on—The Rise, Kingston-on-Thames, in a voice loud enough for Tim to hear.

Then he settled back and patted Rene's hand.

'We'll see it through,' he said. 'Now that we're alone, is there anything else you want to tell me?'

Rene said earnestly: 'Major Dawlish, I'm absolutely convinced of one thing: Alan knows nothing of this. I thought at first he did, and so did my father. We tried to find out what it was about for ourselves because of that. Now we know better, but it's got so hopelessly involved.'

Dawlish patted her hand again as the car sped on.

CHAPTER TWENTY-TWO

THE REAPPEARANCE OF THE DIRECTORS

As the address which Rene had given him was The Rise, Kingston, Dawlish thought wryly that the case was describing a full circle. It had started at Penrod's, and it looked as if it would play to a finish not a mile from the cafe.

He did not speak much on the journey, and the girl sat

tensely beside him.

The drive took a little over half an hour.

The Rise, approached by a narrow lane, was a small house not far from the by-pass. It looked as if it had been a small-holding, but the land had been neglected and the grass, on what might once have been lawns, was knee high.

Dawlish watched carefully.

A low brick wall was on one side of the garden; behind it three or four men could hide with security, and a row of trees could give cover to half a dozen. On the other side, near the by-pass, were clumps of bramble bushes which would also give cover. The little house might have been selected with an eye to delivering a surprise attack.

They were not very far from the camp where Clara Stuart and Mary Hill had been murdered.

The taxi-driver pulled up outside the long, untidy path which led to the house itself.

'Shall I wait, sir?'

'I think you'd better go into Kingston and get some tea,' said Dawlish. 'Be back in half an hour, or a little more.'

The driver set off, and he had almost disappeared from sight when Rene said:

'Are you sure that's wise?'

'Oh, I think so,' said Dawlish. 'After all, we don't want him to see Penrose, do we?'

She sent him a quick, strange look, and then hurried up the path towards The Rise. There was no sign of habitation.

Dawlish knocked on the door. 'Are you sure this is the right place?'

'Of course I'm sure!'

The words were hardly out of her mouth before the door opened, and Penrose stood there.

His face held an anxious, almost frightened look. He waved them inside and then stepped hastily out of sight. Seizing Rene's hands he drew her to him, then turned defensively to Dawlish.

'Dawlish! I know where Lampley and the Halings are, I heard Bloom talking to a dark-haired fellow who seems to know you.'

'Dark lank hair?' asked Dawlish.

'Yes, that describes it. He——'

134

'Never mind about him,' said Dawlish, 'what about the others. Are they safe?'

'So far, yes.' Penrose drew in a deep breath. 'I don't know very much, I only know that you've got to get them away! I daren't go to the police, that's why I asked Rene to send for you. Look here, Dawlish, I knew that I'd been framed. The *real* reason why I didn't say anything is that I—I was afraid that Rene——'

Dawlish smiled dryly.

'Two hearts that suspect as one, is it? Never mind the motives just now, we can worry about them afterwards. Where are the directors?'

'At the company's old factory in North London,' said Penrose rapidly. 'Though it's almost completely destroyed by raids, they've used it from time to time. Bloom discovered that, and he's also been using it for the last few months. I can't go into details now, but——'

Dawlish said: 'I doubt whether you ever will.'

'What do you mean?'

'Look,' said Dawlish.

They were standing in the hall. Doors on either side of them were open and they could see through the windows. Men were advancing on both sides; Dawlish recognised several of those who had been in the raid on Arum Cottage earlier in the day.

Penrose gasped: 'They—they've found us!'

'My dear Alan,' said Dawlish with heavy humour, 'Bloom knew very well that you would try to get in touch with me. He wanted to see me again, so he let you go, as a bait. Now he's sent his men in some strength. There's nothing surprising in it.'

Penrose said: 'But—if you knew——'

'Other men in greater strength will come,' said Dawlish, 'It's only a matter of time, and not much time at that.' He sounded amused. 'You're not used to this kind of business.'

'Thank the Lord I'm not!' exclaimed Penrose, 'but what are you going to do?'

'What can we do?' asked Dawlish.

No one troubled to knock at the door. Someone put a gloved fist through the glass panel, opened it, just as it had been done at Arum Cottage, and came in. Bloom himself followed.

'So it worked,' he said. 'Penrose, you are a bigger fool than I thought you were! As for you, Dawlish——'

135

'There's a certain little proverb which runs: "He laughs best who laughs last", that might, profitably, be called to mind,' said Dawlish airily.

'What do you mean?' rasped Bloom.

'The police——' began Dawlish.

Bloom struck him savagely across the face. The blow made Dawlish reel back against the wall. Bloom glared at him, and then snapped an order.

'Shoot Penrose and the girl, Benn.' He looked at the lank-haired man whom Dawlish had last seen at Greenford Station. 'Don't make any mistake about it this time. As for you, Dawlish, walk straight to those trees. If you try any tricks you'll be shot in the back. Do you understand?'

Dawlish shrugged his shoulders as if he were humouring a child.

Bloom raised his hand as if to strike again, but thought better of it. Dawlish walked stiffly out of the little house. He heard Rene scream and a gasp from Penrose; then there were four shots in quick succession.

He walked towards the trees, accompanied by a cavalcade of armed men, Bloom and the lank-haired man following.

They were half-way there when there was an explosion, and the entire house seemed to split into a dozen pieces. The blast was strong enough to hurl Dawlish heavily to the ground. Bloom had been ready for it, and ducked low; the others had also been prepared, and as Dawlish recovered *he saw that none of them were now covering him.*

Carefully, he crawled further into the trees.

Not until he was almost out of sight did any of them seem to realise that he was gone. There was a snapped word of command, a whispered conversation between the lank-haired man and Bloom, and then a cry of alarm.

'Look there!'

Dawlish could see nothing, but he imagined that they were pointing towards the by-pass and the lane leading to the cottage. He heard the men climbing into their cars and the engines start up.

Flames were now rising from the house. Dawlish observed the smoking wreckage of the place to which Bloom had lured him. He could see Tim approaching, with a taxi-driver, but there was no sign of the police.

Coughing and gasping in the swirls of smoke, Tim pulled up at sight of him.

'Pat!' He drew a deep breath. 'Good God! I thought you were in that inferno!'

'There wasn't much danger, really,' said Dawlish mildly. 'Bloom wanted me to carry back a message, and dead men don't do that, or if they do, it's more often than not the wrong one.'

Tim, staring into the face of his friend, saw that Dawlish was smiling.

From the nearest telephone kiosk, Dawlish telephoned Trivett at the Yard. He told him a little of what he had heard, and suggested that an early inspection of the air-raid shelter at the old factory of Haling & Haling might be useful.

'I was just going to Pymm Place,' Trivett said.

'You can have it watched until you've been to the old factory,' said Dawlish. 'I'll tell you what—or rather *who*—I think you'll find there. Lampley and George and Charles Haling, either trussed up and looking very sorry for themselves, or free and saying that they couldn't get out because the doors were locked from the outside. Of course I may be wrong, but with my usual pig-headedness, I think not.'

'Well, the middle part of your last sentence is proved anyway,' said Trivett heavily.

Dawlish replaced the receiver with a grin.

As he stepped out of the kiosk, Tim said:

'What's on your mind?'

'Tim, I still haven't the foggiest notion of what this business is about,' said Dawlish frankly. 'I imagine that it covers something very big, widespread crimes which have been going on for years, something which matters so much to its promoters that they have thought nothing of murder after murder in order to get what they want. Curious, isn't it? This love of power.' He lit a cigarette while Tim, who was no stranger to Dawlish in this mood, said nothing.

'There has been much confusion, deliberately caused,' went on Dawlish. 'We have been asked to believe a number of incredible things, but it remains a fact that above everything else Bloom wanted Penrose free. To that we have to cling; it is the one definite and clear-cut fact we have. All the rest is irrelevant to the main issue. Bear that in mind when we come to the end, won't you? Don't say that I was wise after the event.'

'What event?' demanded Tim quietly.

'The final disclosure,' said Dawlish with a sudden grin. 'Hallo, there's my cab, on its way back.'

Tim paid off his own driver and they started away just before the first police arrived.

'Where are we going from here?' Tim asked.

'Pymm Place,' said Dawlish.

They reached it in a little more than half an hour. Police were outside, and Dawlish recognised Trivett's car. It looked as if Trivett had decided to visit Wimbledon before going to the air-raid shelter in north London, but as soon as he stepped inside he knew that he was wrong, for Lampley was coming out of a downstairs room. Through the door Dawlish could see the Haling brothers.

Lampley pulled up when he saw Dawlish, and his expression was bleak as he said:

'Where is Rene?'

Dawlish said in a harsh voice: 'The last I saw of her was at a cottage called The Rise, near Kingston. Bloom gave orders for her and Penrose to be shot, and afterwards the cottage was blown sky-high.'

Lampley recoiled as if from a physical blow.

'You—you're not serious!'

'I am,' said Dawlish grimly. 'Where's Trivett?'

'Upstairs,' muttered Lampley.

'Stay down here, Tim,' said Dawlish.

He mounted the stairs two at a time. Trivett's voice was coming from a room at the top, where Sergeant Munk and another were going through a desk. Trivett looked round, and said:

'I'm glad you're here. How did you know where the directors would be?'

'Penrose told me that he had overheard Bloom talking.' He gave Trivett no opportunity to speak, but went on swiftly, describing all that had happened. He spared nothing, and the picture he drew was a graphic one. Even Munk stopped what he was doing and stared at the big man as he listened to the story.

There were movements outside the room, and Lampley and the directors entered. Dawlish finished, with a sharp:

'So what Penrose heard was true. Did you find anything in the air-raid shelter?'

'Nothing of especial interest,' Trivett assured him.

'Of course you did not, because there was nothing of especial interest there,' said George Haling, as if he were reasoning with idiots. 'We used the old shelter as a store place for duplicate records of the company's affairs, that is all. What is this nonsense about Bloom using it?'

'I can only pass on what I was told,' said Dawlish. He paused. 'Have you found anything here, Bill?'

'Not yet.'

'There is nothing here for him to find,' said George Haling. 'I can speak for Lampley, I know the place as well as he does.'

'Do you, indeed,' said Dawlish aggressively. 'Bill'—he looked evenly at Trivett—'if I were you I wouldn't release any one of this trio until you've got to the bottom of the whole business. I don't think any one of them is trustworthy.'

'Don't be absurd!' snapped George. 'We were taken from our homes to the shelter and locked in. I think it is time that some consideration was shown to us, Superintendent——'

There was an exclamation from Charles. Dawlish and the others turned to see Lampley swaying. It looked as if the airman was about to faint. Dawlish moved towards him and at George's directions carried him to his bedroom.

Dawlish uttered no word, but waited while George loosened Lampley's collar and took off his shoes.

'I think we ought to send for Mordaunt,' said Charles agitatedly.

'It's only shock on top of strain,' said George, looking at Dawlish distastefully. 'I have never known a man display such an utter lack of tact or ordinary decency! The way you told him that his daughter was dead was enough to have killed him.'

'Don't talk out of the back of your neck,' said Dawlish rudely. He looked at the man on the bed, then at the Haling brothers, and there was a biting inflection in his voice. 'I wish I could handle you my way, instead of leaving you to the police. I'd find out what little secrets you're hugging to yourselves!'

He turned on his heel and left the room.

As he dialled Mordaunt's number he was smiling faintly.

'Is that Dr. Mordaunt's house? . . . I would like to speak to

Mr. Creem, please. My name is Dawlish.'

'I'm sorry, sir.' A maid answered. 'The gentleman went out, just after you, and didn't return.'

'Oh, did he,' said Dawlish heavily. 'Thank you, good-bye.' He replaced the receiver and looked at Trivett. 'I asked Creem to stay there at all costs. I'm quite sure that he would not have left the place of his own free will. Probably Mordaunt is in this business too, and Creem has discovered it. If that is so, Mordaunt must have put Creem where he can do no harm. How about it?'

'Your suspects are pretty numerous, aren't they?' said Trivett. 'It's time you explained your attitude, Pat. You've behaved like an ill-mannered lout since you came in here, and you haven't done that because you feel bad-tempered. What's on your mind?'

Dawlish said: 'The chief thing on my mind is that I started this business on a false theory, and I feel sore about it. I built it up with the utmost care, and even thought you were a mug for not having done the same thing. The said theory no longer holds. One or more of the people here is concerned. If I were you I would hold them all, I wouldn't just watch them. I'd include Mordaunt too.' He lit a cigarette and went on in a voice pitched so low that there was no likelihood that anyone else could hear him. 'I think I know the real leader of this outfit, and I think I know why those two A.T.S. girls were murdered. I don't know what the business is about, but I think it's pretty grim.'

'If you know the leader, name him,' challenged Trivett.

Dawlish's faint smile played on his lips, and then he said:

'It's Penrose.'

CHAPTER TWENTY-THREE

THE LEADER

EVEN Tim looked sceptical, while Trivett regarded Dawlish with open disapproval.

'Look here, Pat, aren't you getting things a bit tangled up?

You told me yourself that Penrose and the girl had been shot and the house demolished.'

'Not at all,' said Dawlish blandly. 'I said that Bloom ordered someone to shoot Penrose and the girl, but I didn't see the shooting. I heard shots, but I would be extremely surprised if Penrose or Rene were killed.'

Trivett said: 'Seriously?'

'Why should I waste time in flights of fancy?' asked Dawlish. 'Yes, seriously. From the beginning I was sympathetic towards Penrose because it looked as if he were being framed, but I've come to the conclusion that he did murder the first girl, and that the circumstantial evidence was correct. Bloom, who worked for him, waited until it was becoming obvious that the trial would see Penrose convicted before staging the rescue. Remember that the Press took it up pretty strongly, and Bloom grew alarmed. He saw the weight of public opinion going against Penrose, a wave of public indignation which was being stoked up by some of the papers, and he had to act swiftly.'

'But you yourself said——'

'That Penrose was responsible for his own recapture,' said Dawlish, 'and that I believed him when he said that he had hardly known what he was doing when he had been released from Brixton. At the time I really thought that was true. I don't now. I think Penrose knew exactly what he was doing and expected to be rescued. When I followed him, he knew that he had little chance of getting clear. The men in the car with him did not know who he was; they worked for Bloom. So Penrose ratted on them. In effect, he gave himself up. It enabled him to tell a most convincing story of his innocence and his motive for saying little. He even convinced me that he was a modern Sir Galahad, although the more I thought about it the less likely that seemed. He gave some information, *all of which implicated the directors and staff of Haling & Haling.* He seemed extremely reluctant to do that, but his reluctance made it appear even more certain that they were concerned.

'I was beginning to wonder just how genuine he was at Farningham's,' said Dawlish. 'He used the trade mark to load the case against the directors, but to me he seemed to be overdoing it. One thing was only too clear: if he really wanted to conceal the possibility of them being guilty, he would have denied all knowledge of the trade mark.'

'Good Lord!' exclaimed Tim.

Trivett nodded, in agreement with Dawlish.

'Well,' said Dawlish. 'I saw only one way of finding out for certain, and that was to see what happened if he got away. So I passed on the address of Uncle Jerry and he twigged what I was after. The rest speaks for itself, I think. Penrose was so urgently wanted by Bloom that the fat man was prepared to risk his own safety in order to get him free. I was finally convinced of Penrose's complicity when he and Bloom met at Arum Cottage. There was a few minutes of uncertainty, when Bloom really had the wind up. Penrose contrived to make him understand that he was not suspected, and from that moment Bloom became a different man. He had already impressed on me the assurance that he would kill Penrose when he got him, but if that were the case he would have killed him at Arum Cottage.

'However, they weren't sure of themselves. Bloom had worked along the same lines as Penrose, casting blame on the directors. Both of them wanted to know what I thought. So Penrose sent this message to Rene and she passed it on. Then the scene at The Rise was staged. They wanted to convince me that Penrose was dead, and therefore to assume that the directors were the prime movers. They went to a lot of trouble, but they thought it worth it and they think it's succeeded.' He stubbed out his cigarette. 'Well, what do you make of it?'

'How could Penrose direct operations from prison?' Trivett demanded.

'You've explained that. The "padre" was the go-between.'

'I think you're probably right,' said Trivett, drawing a deep breath, 'but I can't see why you've behaved so badly here, Pat. If the directors are being framed, why make out that you still suspect them?'

'Because one of them is probably in it,' said Dawlish.

'Whom do you think?'

'Lampley,' said Dawlish, 'although that's largely guesswork. I don't think he showed any of the right reactions when I told him that his daughter was dead. He only imitated shock symptoms, and that faint was carrying things too far—I don't think he lost consciousness at all. I also think that his daughter was so reticent and worried because she either knows or believes that both her father and her fiancée are as deep in this business as they can be. They may be being forced into it. Whoever telephoned me about Pymm Place put me on the scent while remaining in the background.'

'Rene is alive, too, according to your theory.'

'Yes,' said Dawlish. 'How far one can blame her isn't in my province, Bill. Well, now, what's the situation, assuming that I am right? First, that Penrose and Lampley are in this business together, and that they have knowingly used the company's vans for their purpose. Second, that they persuaded the other directors to try to find out the truth for themselves and so evaded going to the police. The girl probably doped the drinks which sent them all to sleep; the night-watchman, whose evidence might have been awkward, was murdered.

'From there we come to one of the preliminary questions,' went on Dawlish. 'The night-watchman was killed to prevent him from giving evidence against Lampley and the girl and, possibly, Penrose. I imagine that Penrose has been at the company's factory quite a lot since he's been back in England. Well, two A.T.S. girls were killed. Each had the tiny tattoo mark which was originated by Penrose. Ignoring his talk of a trade mark, what does it mean? Bloom was probably nearer the truth when he said that it acted as a kind of password. These two girls then, at one time, helped Penrose or the Penrose organisation. One of them, Clara Stuart, would not go on with it any longer. Penrose said that he quarrelled with her because she would not tell him how she had got the mark. I think he quarrelled with her because she said she was going to make a clean breast of whatever crime she had been condoning or assisting in. Penrose saw only one way of preventing it; he killed her. Later, the other girl discovered why her friend had been killed. The second girl was obviously an associate of Penrose and his people as well, but she probably knew Bloom better than Penrose. Mary Hill, the second girl, had to be killed for the same reason. That all adds up, doesn't it?'

'Yes,' said Trivett slowly.

No one else was near. Even if the Halings were trying to listen from the next floor, Dawlish's voice was pitched on too low a key to let them hear anything.

'Now we come to the fact that Bloom was alarmed because I was in this business,' went on Dawlish. 'That always struck me as being curious. I am known certainly, but only to a limited number. The name Patrick Dawlish is unlikely to strike fear into people of Bloom's calibre. Yet they were upset—so upset that they took great risks, by murdering Carr and trying to murder Laura Desmond. Why?' Dawlish posed the question to himself, and went on gently: 'I am a member of the Intelligence Department. These crimes were committed near an army camp. I imagine that Bloom knew I was in Intelligence *and was alarmed because he thought the Department had made a discovery and was taking an active interest in the murders.*

'Well, Bill, what do you make of it?'

After a long pause, Trivett said:

'You're almost certainly right.' There was an admiring note in his voice.

'There is no other logical explanation of their interest in me and their great anxiety to prevent me finding out what was happening,' said Dawlish. 'Nor is there any other sound reason for their attacks on me. Well, now: we know that the firm is implicated, especially the transport section; we know that Bloom's great fear has been Intelligence Departmental interest. There is a military angle; there is the tattoo mark, probably used as a means of identifying members of this organisation; there is Haling & Haling; there is the use of the vans. Do you remember where Clara Stuart and Mary Hill worked, Bill?'

'Of course, at Kingston. I—oh, I see what you mean,' Trivett broke off, abruptly. 'They were store clerks.'

'Yes,' said Dawlish. 'I think it would be a good idea to have a widespread investigation into the state of army stores up and down the country. Quite a job, don't you think?'

'You'll have to have more grounds for it than you've got,' said Trivett, 'but there might be something in it.'

'That's a concession, at all events,' said Dawlish with a smile. 'Imagine it, Bill, if the Penrose organisation has agents in the stores departments of a number of large camps, agents who can cover up substantial shortages. Imagine, too, how easy it would be for vans to arrive at night, ostensibly to deliver biscuits— perhaps actually delivering biscuits—but also to be loaded up with stolen goods. Imagine what an enormous stock of equipment could be built up over a period of twelve months, for instance, ready for putting on the market as soon as the moment is ripe. That on its own would be big enough, but—arms and ammunition might have disappeared too.'

Trivett said: 'For what purpose?'

'They could be used for quite a lot of things,' said Dawlish. 'They could be smuggled abroad once shipping is decontrolled. They could be used to stir up industrial strife in this country. Of course I may be wrong,' Dawlish went on, with the assurance of one who was quite convinced he was not, 'but I can't get it out of my head that stores have probably been disappearing on a large scale, and they've been tucked away somewhere. *If* this sign is widely used, *if* there are agents of the Penrose organisation in many army camps, then there are a lot of people involved. Hundreds, possibly thousands. I think that Penrose and Bloom have been building up stocks and supplies to feed and clothe a large number of men after things have settled down in this country. I can't imagine what they propose to do, but I don't like the thought of several hundred armed men, who can pose as soldiers, at liberty in England. Do you?'

'It would certainly be a very dangerous state of affairs,' said Trivett with prim disapproval.

'Well, one thing is obvious,' Dawlish went on, 'these stores go somewhere. They must take up a lot of room. There is a place next to the factory at Greenford—a shadow factory. The company is supposed to be keeping it ready until they can start expanding, when it will be put into production. I wonder what it's being used for now?'

'We can soon find out,' said Trivett grimly.

'Don't start too soon,' said Dawlish. 'Let's try to find out whether there has been any jiggery-pokery at the Kingston camp, for instance—and, say, take three other camps in the south and have a complete investigation into the stores positions. I can arrange it, I think.'

'What about the Greenford factory?'

'Have it closely watched,' said Dawlish. 'I once thought that this house might be used to keep the records, but you've found nothing here, you say?'

'Not yet,' said Trivett.

'As there seems no great alarm among the people upstairs, you probably won't,' said Dawlish. 'Mordaunt's house is another possible hiding place. Tim and I can do that, and we'll get Napier. Felicity can get out to Kingston and start things there. If you'll make a report to the A.C., Bill, and get his reactions, that should be a big help. I'll also have a word with Whitehead before I go to Mordaunt's place,' he added. 'I'll use a telephone kiosk, I think.'

He went along the road to the kiosk which he had used once before, and spoke first to Felicity. She would have no difficulty, she said, in checking up on the stores position at Kingston. She confirmed that the A.T.S. staff handled most of the work and that the two murdered girls had been overseers at the store.

Dawlish put in a call to his own Chief, and Colonel Whitehead, a man who rarely wanted a thing explained twice, listened with great attention. When Dawlish had finished, he said:

'You might be right, Dawlish. I'll arrange for an inspection of stores at half a dozen camps, it won't be difficult and it isn't unusual enough to attract much attention.'

'Good,' said Dawlish, heartily. 'What matters, of course, is to make sure that the actual supplies tally with the stock records. If they don't, it will be easy. If they do, then all requisitions for goods will have to be checked, to make sure that the signatures on them are genuine. But I don't think I need to tell you about that, sir!'

'Nor do I, Dawlish,' said Whitehead dryly, 'nor do I!'

The man named Bloom shifted his bulk in the large armchair in which he was sitting, and looked across the narrow, low-ceilinged room at Penrose. There was an air of assurance about Penrose which Dawlish had never seen, although Bloom himself looked ill-at-ease. Rene Lampley, at a small desk covered with manilla folders, was flushed and agitated.

It was twenty-four hours after Dawlish had persuaded the authorities to start the inspection of the stores.

'So it would appear that we were right to be wary of Dawlish,' said Penrose in a thin voice. 'Even when I saw him I did not believe that he had any idea of what we are doing, but now there is no doubt. The authorities will have a shock when they discover how much is missing,' he added with a humourless smile.

'Now listen to me,' Bloom said, 'we've got to do something, it's not anything to laugh about.' He spoke jerkily, as if he were out of breath. 'If you hadn't killed that girl——'

'Both girls had to be killed,' said Penrose. 'We wouldn't have had a chance otherwise.'

'A fine chance we've got now!' snapped Bloom.

'I am coming to the conclusion that you are a white-livered

skunk,' said Penrose dispassionately. 'You were brave enough when things were going well, but now we're in trouble you're showing yourself for what you're worth.'

Bloom licked his lips.

'Well, what can we do?'

'If needs be, fight it out,' said Penrose. 'We ourselves will probably be able to get away. Need I remind you that even if we were to die, we shall not have failed?' There was a glint in his eyes, and he did not look quite normal. 'Up and down the country there are dumps of arms and ammunition and army clothes, in the country there are quite enough men to wear those clothes and use those arms. When the fools in Whitehall think the war is over, then we shall strike!' His voice was rising, and he seemed almost to have forgotten that the others were present.

Bloom watched him with narrowed eyes, but Rene Lampley stood up, slowly, as if she could not believe her ears.

'*What* did you say?' she demanded.

Penrose glanced at her.

'Don't be alarmed, my dear! I——'

'What do you mean by "we shall strike"? I thought——'

Penrose interrupted her smoothly.

'You and your father thought that I pictured myself as a kind of Robin Hood, ready to take advantage of the chaos that there will be in this country after the war. How wrong you were! It was never true that I planned only a series of highway robberies and bank hold-ups, although I let you think it. You see, I needed your help, and I knew that you would be too squeamish to work for the Cause. The Cause, do you hear me?'

She stood rigid, without speaking.

'I have been planning and working on this for years!' Penrose went on. 'Undermining! Tunnelling! Ferreting. Bah! If I had my way there would not be anything of England left but dirt and rubble and corpses! England!' He spat against the wall, banged a clenched fist on the desk and shouted: 'I hate the name, I hate every man and woman who is English! Once I thought that The Leader would come here, once I thought that my preparations would help him set the seal to his colossal victory but now——'

'Don't!' cried Rene, 'don't go on!'

'You have a remarkably thin skin'—Penrose laughed with sour bitterness—'for one who had no objection to living in luxury on the profits from widespread burglaries and robberies, or to being a party to murder. Yet you pretend that you have a conscience, you pretend that because I am fighting for a Cause that it is despicable. Listen to me, my dear! I was born in Germany of an English father and a German mother. I spent my childhood in Germany, and it was there that I was given a sacred task by The Leader, a task that will be fulfilled! I have organised men to use the arms which have been stolen. When England thinks that peace is here again, then those men will strike, whether I live or die. They will destroy, destroy, destroy! Factories, mines, railways and power stations, gasworks and reservoirs—never will there have been such a rain of destruction in the history of mankind! For every place in Germany destroyed by English bombs there will be a sweet revenge!'

He paused, licking his lips. Rene stared at him, as if horror-struck. Bloom was clenching and unclenching his hands.

Penrose went on as if intoning a hymn of hate:

'When the country is mad with joy, celebrating its so-called victory, when the watch is relaxed and precautions forgotten, then we will strike. Against such a destiny what does the life or death of a few men and women count? *You* understand that, Bloom, don't you?' he added, looking coldly at the fat man.

'We—we don't want to throw our lives away,' Bloom muttered.

'Ah, so now we have it. The unmasking of a poltroon, and a hypocrite!' He looked at Rene.

She drew in her breath, as if it hurt her.

'Are you—are you sure that he did not know?'

'If by "he" you mean your father, he had no idea of what I was really planning. Bloom had, and one or two others, but not the Lampleys. I——'

He broke off, for the telephone rang. He answered it quickly. Then replaced the receiver.

'It appears that your father has escaped from Pymm Place and will be here in a few minutes. We will see whether he will be as shocked as his daughter. It should be interesting.'

There was silence in the room for a few minutes, and then a door opened and Lampley came in. He was dishevelled and he looked tired, but there was a smile on his face.

'Father!' Rene burst out, 'they——'

'Don't break the news so suddenly,' said Penrose. 'Come in,

Lampley! We are in some trouble, because Dawlish is getting results from his inquiries and we shall almost certainly be raided. It is worrying Bloom and your daughter. I have been reassuring them that, no matter what happens to us, the Cause will prosper.'

'Cause?' repeated Lampley, as if startled.

'We mustn't let him go on!' Rene gasped, 'we must make him tell us just where the dumps are, we must stop it!'

'I see what you mean,' said Lampley. 'Yes, I see what you mean, but—after all, Rene——' He gave a little unnatural laugh. 'It's not so very different, we knew that we would be stirring up a lot of trouble. Don't let it worry you, my dear, it is only a difference in degree.'

'You're more of a realist than I expected,' Penrose said.

'What else can I be?' asked Lampley. 'I heard Dawlish telling one of his friends that they are going to raid the shadow factory tomorrow.'

'Tomorrow!' exclaimed Bloom.

'Yes, we haven't much time,' Lampley said urgently. 'We can get to the main factory, of course, and the hall is on ground level. Er——' he broke off, looking at Penrose, while Rene stood there with her face chalk-white.

'What were you going to say?' demanded Penrose.

'Supposing we get through and you don't,' said Lampley, 'how—er—how am I going to make sure that I get the—er—reward? You weren't going to do this for nothing, were you?'

Penrose said: 'You're certainly a realist! You'd better get me out safely, Lampley, to make sure that you can live on the fat of the land afterwards!'

'You're mad!' Rene gasped, 'you're all mad! Even if you get away now you'll be hunted all your life, you'll never get out of the country. We've been discovered, it's too late to save ourselves but we can—we can stop him from this terrible thing! Daddy, we must!'

Her father stared at her without expression.

She drew in her breath, and then suddenly swung to the desk and pulled open a drawer. Lampley cried: 'Stop that!' Penrose moved swiftly and as the girl pulled an automatic from the desk he struck her across the face. The girl went staggering back against the wall, and the gun dropped to the floor.

Penrose picked it up.

'Listen, Lampley. If you get through and I don't, get in touch with the woman Desmond, Mrs. Laura Desmond, do you understand? She will be able to help you. She has all the particulars of the locations of the dumps, the men who will work with us, and she knows everything.'

'Desmond!' gasped Bloom. 'Why, I thought——'

'You thought Smythe went to kill her,' said Penrose, 'but you were wrong. I gave Smythe orders through the "padre". He was to make it appear as if he planned to murder Mrs. Desmond, but actually his task was to make sure that she could not be suspected. She had gone to Penrod's to keep an eye on Dawlish, and find out if he were working for his Department,' continued Penrose. 'You were right to kill Carr, Bloom, it would have been fatal if he had been questioned, for he would have wanted to work with Dawlish and we could not risk having a friend of Dawlish's a friend of Laura's also. You were wrong to think that killing Carr would prevent them from finding the address in Putney. I told Smythe to carry that letter, so as to give away the Putney address, but I also arranged that he should die before he could get really frightened and talk too much. You see how cleverly it had been done, Lampley?'

'Yes,' said Lampley. 'I—er—there's one other thing. I think Dawlish is interested in Mordaunt. I got some poison from Mordaunt's. It is the same that the dog so inadvertently ate, and brings instant death. I gave it to one of our men who, I understand, used it for Creem. We can't stop the police and military concentrating, of course, but I wanted to cause as many distractions as I could.'

'You're a better man than I thought you were,' said Penrose approvingly. 'All right, we'll get to work on details. We'll arrange for the vans to be loaded from here tomorrow night, of course, and——'

He went into some detail; by arranging for the vans to be driven away in an effort to break down the barricades which would be put up round the factory, he hoped to make Dawlish and the authorities think that the only stores in his possession were at the shadow factory. All that mattered, he said, was to prevent anyone from suspecting that there were dumps up and down the country.

'They won't learn that,' Lampley said. 'Come and lend me a hand, will you?'

'I'll follow,' said Penrose. 'Go with Lampley, Bloom.'

When he was alone with Rene, who lay on the floor, unconscious, he stared at her huddled body for some time without speaking. Then he snapped his fingers, went to a drawer in the desk and drew out a hypodermic syringe. He filled it from a small bottle, wrapped the needle carefully in cotton wool, and tucked it away in his waistcoat pocket.

Then he stood looking down at the girl again.

'There's more in your father than I thought there was,' he said, 'but I don't think he would stand for you being killed.' He smiled thinly, and went on in a whispering voice: 'A shot from this before you leave tomorrow and another shot for Bloom, will see you both dead in a few minutes. If your father and I get through, he'll be reliable enough. If we don't——'

He drew himself up to attention then suddenly flung out his hand, and his voice rang through the room. 'Heil Hitler!'

The expression in his eyes as he went out was not sane. The girl remained huddled there, unconscious.

At six o'clock that evening Creem's body was found behind a hedge on Wimbledon Common. It was soon apparent that he had been poisoned, and within half an hour Mordaunt was being questioned. The police surgeon in charge searched Mordaunt's dispensary, finding a phial of the poison which had been used on Creem as well as on Beresford. According to notes left with the preparations, the stuff would cause a condition approximating gangrene in a very quick time.

Mordaunt declared that he had made the discovery while trying to find a much quicker and safer way of dealing with open wounds. He did not protest his innocence too strongly, and denied all knowledge of the activities of Haling & Haling. He agreed that Lampley had persuaded him and the Haling brothers not to ask for police help with the van mystery, but declared that he did not think that there had been any ulterior motive in that.

Dawlish was there when he was questioned.

'You were talking to Lampley on the day when I first met you,' said Dawlish. 'What was it about?'

'This business,' said Mordaunt wearily. 'We often discuss the affairs of the company. I thought that Lampley was most unhappy about the vans business, and he was asking me that

151

evening not to make any statement about it, in view of what had happened.'

'I see,' said Dawlish. 'Do you know where he is now?'

'I thought that he was being watched by the police,' said Mordaunt.

'He was,' said Dawlish, 'but he got away.'

It was true that Lampley had disappeared and equally true that no one knew where he had gone. There were no reports from the police watching the factory, but there might be a secret way in. That was a thing which worried Dawlish. He had expected Lampley to make his bid for freedom on the following night after he had talked of an attack on the Greenford factory. He had also talked of it in the hearing of the Halings, but they had not made any attempt to get away.

Dawlish was most concerned about where the stores would be found.

That they were missing was now proved beyond doubt, and an increasing and imposing list was discovered. Moreover, over one hundred men and women, some civilians and some service staff, had been found with the tattoo mark which had first been seen on the shoulders of the murdered A.T.S. The general alarm certainly seemed justified.

At ten o'clock that night Dawlish, Tim and Napier were in the Brook Street flat, with Felicity. Napier had only just heard of Creem's death, and he was badly shaken. He was also anxious to find some way of avenging it, and he listened intently as Dawlish said:

'If they're at Greenford, and Lampley was warned them that we shall make a raid tomorrow, they will probably try to get the stuff out tonight. The police will be there in strength and there will be several companies of infantry. We might have little trouble, but they'll probably make a fight of it. Is that clear?'

'Yes,' said Napier.

'We want Penrose, Lampley, Bloom and the girl,' said Dawlish. 'There may be some doubt about Rene, but none whatever about Lampley. We want them alive, if we can arrange it.' He spoke quite dispassionately, while looking at Napier. 'We don't know how widespread this thing might be, and that we must find out. All understood?'

'Yes,' said Tim, and Napier nodded.

'Then we'll get off,' said Dawlish. 'Oh, I nearly forgot Elmer

Wright.'

He telephoned the Agency and warned Wright to go to Greenford; Wright was elated. Dawlish kissed Felicity after the others had gone into the hall. She did not speak, so many good-byes, she thought, and one, perhaps this one, will be the last.

A police car was waiting for Dawlish outside.

When he reached Greenford, the police and military were already there in strength. All the roads were blocked to traffic coming into the area.

'We're not far wrong,' Trivett said, 'we've stopped several lorries, and their drivers were going to pick up loads at the factory. Army equipment mostly.' He gave details.

Dawlish nodded with satisfaction.

'We'll stay fairly near the doors of the main factory,' he said. 'I fancy our bunch will try to come out that way.'

They took up their position inside the gates, which were open. Behind them was stretched a net of stout rope.

The night was very quiet. From the grounds of the factory, just after midnight, there came the sound of engines being revved up, and the faint murmur of voices travelled across. At half-past twelve, the first van came out.

The police and military allowed it to go as far as a barrier two miles further on, where it was stopped. The driver and his companion were overpowered without any trouble, and said that at least twenty vans and a dozen lorries were waiting to be loaded. It was found to be loaded with machine-guns and small arms.

The second and third vans followed the fate of the first.

So far, there was no suspicion inside the shadow factory, no hint of trouble, but when the fourth van came out its driver, warned by a careless movement on the part of one of the police, suddenly accelerated and crashed through the barrier. Dawlish did not know that inside it there was a radio-operator, who flashed word back to the factory.

Then the fifth van came out.

Suddenly, without warning, it put on speed, and men from the driver's cabin and the back opened fire with machine-guns. The van roared along the road, a sixth and a seventh van fol-lowed swiftly.

'Here it comes,' Dawlish said.

He heard the police and military giving orders and he saw men approaching the factory, some of them in small tanks and armoured cars. The shooting which started from the building itself showed the determination with which the defenders would fight. The night was suddenly rent with the flash of flames and the sharp crack of explosions.

The defenders were well-placed, and the first attack was repulsed. As the men went back for cover, Napier muttered:

'If we're not darned careful, they'll get away with it.'

'Not on your life!' said Dawlish.

The men regrouped and went into the attack again, this time more cautiously. The shooting was less irregular, and there was no wild attack. A heavier gun opened up from the front of the shadow factory, and the guns of a medium-sized tank opened up in reply.

Dawlish waited by the entrance of the main building, banking on the chance that Bloom and Penrose and the others would try to get out that way. The tension ran high.

Searchlight batteries had been brought up and were flood-lighting the immediate area. Others were being put into position to cover the main factory.

Suddenly there was the roar of an explosion between Dawlish's party and the main factory doors. Debris hurtled through the air and crashed about them.

'Careful, now! Don't fire yet, we want 'em alive,' Dawlish muttered.

He suspected that the four leaders of the organisation had tried to blast a way clear, and hardly were the words out of his mouth when he heard the sharp staccato roar of a motor-cycle. It tore through the open doors of the factory, and was away. Dawlish saw it clearly as a searchlight, suddenly put into action, flood-lit the whole scene. He could see into the hall which he had visited so short a time before. Other motor-cycles were there, some with riders, some about to be ridden.

The second roared out into the night.

Suddenly a shell from the heavy gun struck the searchlight nearest Dawlish. As the light went out the glass shattered and the men near it fell. At the same time the third motor-cycle roared towards Dawlish. It was happening so quickly that there seemed a chance that the daring attempt would succeed.

Then a queer thing happened.

Bloom was roaring towards them, with Rene Lampley close behind him, and for a few brief seconds there was no firing.

Then one after the other the cyclists lost control and crashed. There seemed no reason for it; they had not been wounded, but, half-way between the factory and the net, machines and riders toppled to the ground.

The third cyclist came on; he was Lampley.

By then police were hurrying towards the new danger spot. Lampley zig-zagged right and left, and remained unhurt until his machine crashed into the net. He went flying off, the cycle crashed and turned over.

Penrose came last.

He tried new tactics; Dawlish thought that he had seen the net and knew what to expect. He slowed down, without warning, and then leapt from his machine and raced for the netting; obviously he meant to jump clear.

Dawlish went for him.

Both men fired, then crashed into each other. Dawlish reeled back from the collision, while Penrose fell heavily. Police and military were at the spot in force, now.

Napier and the police went to the assistance of Penrose, and of Lampley.

Both Rene and Bloom were dead.

It was so strange for neither appeared to be injured.

'I don't like it,' Trivett said, 'I fancy they were poisoned before they left, and died as they rode. The same business that was worked with Smythe.' He bent over Rene again, noting the contracted pupil. 'And I can guess why; Penrose didn't want either of them caught alive.'

'So there's still something we don't know,' Dawlish said, grimly. 'I wonder if——'

'Daw-lish!' Napier called, standing over the body of Lampley. 'He's trying to talk.'

Dawlish went down on one knee beside the injured man. The glare of the headlights showed Lampley's face clearly, the strain at his eyes and the desperate effort he was making to talk. Yet his words were hardly audible. Dawlish, convinced that there was something which he did not know, felt a sense of desperate urgency. Yet his hands were gentle when he pressed Lampley back to the ground, and his voice was low-pitched and even.

'Take it easy, now, don't rush it.'

Lampley said: 'Dawlish——' He stopped, then tried again. 'Laura—Desmond. List of—dumps—all over the—country.' He stopped again, and then gasped: 'Can you—hear me?'

'Yes,' said Dawlish in a strained voice. His mind was filled with confusion, and a steadfast determination to understand why Lampley was talking.

Lampley seemed to gain momentarily in strength.

'Dawlish, I didn't know what was behind it. Thought it was a plan to—cash in on the boom after the war. No objection to that. Didn't know Penrose was—a Nazi.'

Dawlish exclaimed: *'Penrose!'*

'Yes. Man was—mad! Aimed to cause chaos when the war was over. Everything organised. Get Laura Desmond. Only person with all details. Dawlish!'

'Take it easy now,' Dawlish repeated gently.

'Rene—didn't know. I didn't. Managed to find out about Desmond tonight. Listen! When I first—when I first——' Lampley paused, and then went on: 'When I first suspected the truth I telephoned you, said I was Blossom, gave you the address of Pymm Place. Hoped you would find out—— Hoped——'

He stopped again, for the last time.

It was very dark in the hall of Laura Desmond's flat.

Dawlish was standing outside her drawing-room; he had forced the front door without much trouble. Napier was behind him and the police were within call. The grimness of Dawlish's expression was not assumed; he could not get over the shock of learning that the woman here was a party to the crimes, that he had been so completely hoodwinked.

Gently, Dawlish opened the door.

There was a single reading-lamp in the room, and he could see the woman sitting on a settee. She had not heard him. He watched her for some seconds and then stepped boldly into the room.

'Good evening!' he said. 'Penrose is caught, and has talked.'

He had never seen such an expression on a woman's face, such a look of malignancy in eyes which had always been so fluttery, the eyes of a coquette. In that single, vivid moment he realised that she was a brilliantly clever woman, fully capable of carrying on the work which Penrose had started.

She stared at him, but her right hand moved towards her handbag. He stood there empty-handed, as if he were alone. She pulled the bag towards her and opened it, trying to make it seem casual. Then, after a long pause, she said in her light voice:

'Why, *Major* Dawlish! *What* did you say?'

'I said that Penrose had talked,' said Dawlish.

Then she got the bag open and he put his hand in his pocket, with a movement so quick that he had his gun out before she had hers. He did not waste time, but fired at her wrist; the bullet shattered it. She did not cry out, but her hand dropped to her side.

He took a step towards her, and then she flung herself at him.

Mrs. Laura Desmond would be weak for some days, said the doctors, and her wrist would never be normal again, but she would not die from the wound.

Hidden in various parts of the flat were the names and addresses of factories and shops which had been rented for the storing of arms and ammunition, hand-grenades, Mills bombs and a dozen other explosive weapons, together with incendiaries and land mines, cylinders of liquid fire, everything that would be necessary for the campaign of violence which had been planned.

There was evidence that the organisation had been built up over many years. When questioned, the majority of the conspirators declared that they had first been bribed to supply small quantities of arms and then been blackmailed into increasing the quantities.

None knew anything of the true scale on which the weapons had been stolen, all believed that they worked in the only depot concerned—except the small band of picked men who had operated the lorries. The goods had been taken first to Greenford and then distributed to the various dumps.

Dawlish and Trivett were in the Superintendent's room at Scotland Yard, several days after the final act at Greenford. Trivett looked tired, for he had been working almost without respite on the case. Now, he said, they had everything they could expect to find.

'We can't complain,' said Dawlish. 'Lampley, his daughter, Bloom and Penrose were all working well together, on the post-war gangster idea: it wasn't until Lampley discovered something deeper that they really got into trouble—except, of course, for

Penrose's arrest. That must have shaken them!'

'The man was a consummate actor,' Trivett said.

Dawlish grimaced.

'Not to speak of Laura Desmond! Anyhow, Lampley got his way. He hoped to keep clear, of course. Bloom and Penrose were planning to implicate all the directors of the company, so as to distract attention from themselves, and also to implicate Mordaunt. Oh, it was neatly done! Lampley wanted me to roam round the factory, of course. Probably Bloom was there at the time and sent Lank Hair after me—did you find that customer, by the way?'

'He was one of the lorry drivers who was killed.'

'Good! Well, we can see now how it all worked. The real cause of the collapse of this pretty show was the arrest of Penrose, Bill. Your trick!'

'I'll call it evens,' said Trivett. 'Tell me, Pat, if Lampley hadn't talked, would you have thought of Mrs. Desmond?'

'No,' said Dawlish. 'A grim fact for me to remember.'

He was in sombre mood as he went back to the flat, but when he saw Felicity, alone, and without any shadow of anxiety in her eyes, he cheered up.

'All over and done with,' he said, hugging her, 'and doubt whether we'll have any more alarms, my sweet, the Nazi Locker must be pretty empty by now. A quiet, family life will be our rule from now on!'

'You're joking, of course,' said Felicity, laughing. 'I don't think you could live without danger, darling!'

'See who's talking,' declared Dawlish indignantly. 'Who got me into it? I know what: Let's advertise: "Happily married couple, experienced in dangerous projects, will accept any commission leading to excitement. Payment no object." How does that sound?'

'Horrible!' declared Felicity. 'You've forgotten Ted, Tim and Napier!'

TWO SHOCKING THRILLERS
BY BRIAN CLEEVE

VOTE X FOR TREASON

The story of a desperate man. They had him paroled
out of prison to do their dirty work. And they told
him he would stay out—IF.
The job was dangerous: to infiltrate a neo-Fascist
group planning blackmail and political ju jitsu. But
it was the assignment within the assignment that had
him worried—it was more hideously dangerous than
he had bargained for.
552 08146 9   4/-

THE JUDAS GOAT

A horror story, a study in sadism, that is told as
a counter-intelligence suspense story. A Cabinet
Minister is threatened with exposure of a very nasty
secret in his past. An Irish Terrorist, trained in killing,
a hard tough man, is used by the Secret Service. But
he is not quite tough enough for the sickening work
to which he is assigned.
552 08147 7   4/-

CORGI BOOKS
A DIVISION OF TRANSWORLD PUBLISHERS

A SELECTION OF
SPY AND CRIME BOOKS
UNDER THE CORGI BANNER

Spy Thrillers

☐	07872 7	THE KREMLIN LETTER		
☐	07855 7	STRIP TEASE	Noel Behn	5/-
☐	07754 2	COLD SPELL	Jean Bruce	3/6
☐	07737 2	SHORT WAVE	Jean Bruce	3/6
☐	07413 8	POLE REACTION	Jean Bruce	3/6
☐	08032 2	DOOMSDAY ENGLAND	Jean Bruce	3/6
☐	08004 7	MADRIGAL	Michael Cooney	5/-
☐	07905 7	HIDEAWAY	John Gardner	5/-
☐	07716 X	AMBER NINE	John Gardner	3/6
☐	07463 2	UNDERSTRIKE	John Gardner	3/6
☐	07224 9	THE LIQUIDATOR	John Gardner	3/6
☐	07907 3	THE EXPENDABLE SPY	John Gardner	3/6
☐	07687 2	THE MAN WHO SOLD DEATH	Jack D. Hunter	5/-
☐	07677 5	DIE RICH DIE HAPPY	James Munro	3/6
☐	08062 4	THE MONEY THAT MONEY CAN'T BUY	James Munro	3/6
			James Munro	5/-

Crime

☐	07623 6	DEADFALL	Desmond Cory	3/6
☐	08170 1	INVITATION TO ADVENTURE	John Creasey	3/6
☐	07832 8	AN AXE TO GRIND	A. A. Fair (Erle Stanley Gardner)	3/6
☐	07697 X	CUT THIN TO WIN	A. A. Fair (Erle Stanley Gardner)	3/6
☐	07038 6	TRY ANYTHING ONCE	A. A. Fair (Erle Stanley Gardner)	3/6
☐	08033 0	MISTER SCIPIO	Tudor Gates	3/6
☐	07973 1	THE BODY LOVERS	Mickey Spillane	4/-
☐	07831 X	THE BY-PASS CONTROL	Mickey Spillane	3/6
☐	07753 4	THE TWISTED THING	Mickey Spillane	3/6
☐	08223 6	THE DELTA FACTOR	Mickey Spillane	4/-
☐	08179 5	VENGEANCE IS MINE	Mickey Spillane	4/-
☐	08180 9	THE FLIER	Mickey Spillane	4/-
☐	08181 7	KILLER MINE	Mickey Spillane	4/-
☐	08182 5	THE DEEP	Mickey Spillane	4/-
☐	07606 6	RETURN OF THE HOOD	Mickey Spillane	3/6
☐	08081 0	THE COLOUR OF MURDER	Julian Symons	4/-
☐	08080 2	BLAND BEGINNING	Julian Symons	4/-
☐	08079 9	THE KILLING OF FRANCIE LAKE	Julian Symons	4/-
☐	08229 5	THE PROGRESS OF A CRIME	Julian Symons	4/-